PRAISE FOR CHARLENE ELSBY

"A fascinating, sometimes dizzying look at the narratives we build out of other people and what they build upon us. Sometimes you have to revel in the obsessive weirdness of the world. Elsby turns the skull into a cubicle for the mind."

— HAILEY PIPER, AUTHOR OF *A GAME IN YELLOW*

Charlene's latest is a taut and terrifying journey through a horrific world of conformists---office people who seek to normalize all things into best practices. At stake is a life worth living. At play are all of modern-life's biggest mysteries: What does it mean to be an individual in increasingly homogenized societies? Why does individuality give us hope? Does my cat even like me?

If Kafka had set out to write *A Brave New World*, the result would be a story like this. Clever and terrifying. Charlene Elsby is an artist.

— BRIAN ALLEN CARR, AUTHOR OF *OPIOID, INDIANA*

"Pitch black humor meets the existential dread of contemporary corporate culture in this tour de force from Elsby. Surreal, hilarious, and heartbreaking all at once, you'll keep going despite the pain, like a cancer-ridden lung wheezing out another smoky laugh. A must-read if you've ever been ensnared in bureaucratic hell."

THE ORGANIZATION
IS HERE TO SUPPORT YOU

CHARLENE
ELSBY

WEIRD
PUNK

CONTENTS

PART ONE

1

I LOOK AT THE LIGHT ON MY TOP LEFT MONITOR, BREATHING. It's asleep. Someone went to the trouble to put a light on the power button that grows in intensity, until it reaches a maximum, and then it begins an alternate process, ultimately fading to darkness. It's smooth and consistent, each breath in the same length as each breath out. You'll never catch it stuck, out of air, waiting that extra second before it takes its next inhale—not like when you're sleeping next to another person, and every so often, for a part of a second, they pause, and you think, there's a chance they've breathed everything out, and that this time the cycle won't start again—until it does. Another death evaded, and another one the next moment. The light on the monitor doesn't mimic breath, it mocks it, trying to show how easy it is, when a human, any human, at any given moment, just might fail to go on inhaling and exhaling. The monitor keeps on, antagonizing life and its imperfections, feigning sleep, when it might as well be death. The monitor has never seen anything die. It doesn't know how dependent it is on me to let it go on, keep breathing. But I pay its power bills. I'm the one with *anima*. Each morning, I consider whether to wake it up, once again, like all the days before, or to unplug it, throw it out the window, watch the cars try to avoid it on the road, until one of them finally hits it, ridding me of it forever.

Each morning, so far, I've awakened it. But each morning may be the morning I might not.

Maurice, when he was around, used to argue that employment is a constraint. I *have to* log in. I *have to* perform. I do not *choose* which tasks I complete. I have been bought, he'd say, if he knew where I lived and worked now.

But Maurice didn't know what it's like to be really constrained. He'd never needed something he didn't have. *Having everything you need*, I told him. *That's freedom.* And since not all of us are born rich, we have to work. *At least*, I would tell him, if I were arguing with him now, *at least now I can decide whether or not to go without.* At least now I can walk down the hall and buy a Diet Coke, if I want one—*whenever I want one.* Such a thing seemed so impossible for so long, and Maurice didn't even consider it, didn't know what that was like, had heard of it, certainly, but didn't really believe in it, that there were people in the situation of not being able to have a soda whenever they so choose—and certainly not me. I was pretty, and I was smart. Surely someone would give me everything I need. *That's not how it works, Maurice*, I'd say, exasperated.

This is not constraint. Constraint is when someone demands the impossible of you and denies you something you need when you can't meet that demand. It means you always need something. I, on the other hand, as long as I keep showing up, will always have everything I need. *That's freedom, Maurice.*

I continue to argue with my memories of Maurice as I wait until eight thirty.

Freedom is being assured that every moment before eight thirty is my own time, and they won't have any of it. Even though I'm in the workspace area of my unit, early again (why do I keep waking up earlier and earlier?), I let the machines sleep until eight thirty. I have to be careful. If I start logging on earlier, they'll come to expect it. I set eight thirty as a start time, because I used to sleep much later, used to be awake much later, but ever since I started working at these machines, I'm tired so much faster, sleeping much more efficiently, and then awake again before I'd ever want to be. My colleagues log in earlier, some at seven thirty, some at seven, some at six in the morning, but those last ones, I doubt them. How would they have the time before to shower, have a coffee, prepare for the day? They must be logging on as they roll out of bed, moving the mouse around between brushing their teeth and brushing their hair, making it seem like they're at work already when really, there's nothing yet to do. We all get to log off eight hours exactly from when we log in, so if you log in at six in the morning, you can log off at two in the afternoon. I, on the other hand, am around until four thirty. By four thirty, everyone else is gone and, just like at six am, there's nothing to do. But sometimes, once in a while, there's someone left, clocking in overtime on a project that there just weren't enough hours in the day to finish, and sometimes, I'll even get a message from them, at which point I get to respond, promptly and diligently, with some response that answers whatever they asked of me, but which really says, "I'm still here."

After four thirty, it's my time again. Let the monitors sleep their inhuman sleep, all evening and all night. There's always the chance that if I turned them on, something would be there to do, something important, something that can't wait until morning.

How can they not wake up, knowing all that?

But they don't.

Even if they did, better them than me.

2

TODAY OF ALL DAYS, IT IS IMPORTANT TO BE PUNCTUAL. FOR today is my annual performance review. Each year, the stakeholders take part in the collaborative process of determining the quality of my performance. I and my immediate supervisor, along with her immediate supervisor, attempt to recall what it is I've done all year, and to reduce that into a one-page summary that can be easily digested by those whose positions rank them even higher. I am a level 07 officer. If I succeed in my tasks for a number of years, I will inevitably become a level 08 officer. To become a level 09, 10, 11, I must leave the realm of officers entirely, become something else, another classification altogether—analyst, advisor, specialist, executive. But I do not want to. I do not want to do that.

I do not want to be promoted so far up that I am alone.

I take solace in how many officers there are and how, in the event of an emergency, another one of me would take my place. There would be no interruption in service. My files would become someone else's files. I've seen it so many times already. Someone whose work is necessary and important falls out of circulation and—all of a sudden—someone else whose work is also necessary and important comes to take their place. The email signature changes, but the production doesn't cease.

At level 07, we are all one and the same, and that's how it ought to be.

The more of me there are, the better.

After today, I expect my work to continue as usual.

Because the years don't stop for the evaluations. The work continues, unceasing, the day-by-day not broken but instead enforced by the annual performance review that at once sums up my existence, but also justifies it and, by doing so, confirms that not only am I performing well, but am being used efficiently by my superiors, as a resource for the organization. It's as much their performance review as mine. After all, if I weren't performing adequately, why haven't my mentors ensured that I have the opportunities to develop the capacities I might need to thrive? Why has the organization failed to encourage my potential, to maximize my aptitudes, to apply my valuable skill set to the problems that plague society today?

We are all *satisfactory*.

My first supervisor informed me, early in the contract, that we are all satisfactory. We are not good, or excellent, or very good, and never *un*satisfactory, but all and always satisfactory. "Don't let it get you down," she said. "They're always satisfactory."

"I don't pin my self-worth on this job," I had said.

And she nodded, approvingly.

Because here, we are all excellent all year round, and we are all satisfactory when it comes time to measure that excellence. We know that to excel, we must not think ourselves better than any other. We all work hard, and we all perform, and because of our excellent performances, we are all satisfactory. To be satisfactory in the organization is to have succeeded. To want for more is to betray our colleagues, whose work we might be implying to be inferior to our own. *It is not*. A colleague's failure to thrive *cannot* be attributed to a personal failing; it is, as we say, a failure of the organization to recognize and encourage the individual's potential in relevant ways.

Every individual is an infinite potential.

8

It is against every rule of decency to differentiate between us, and especially if that differentiation is an attempt to distinguish a better from *a worse*.

It is against the collective agreement.

When at the end of the fiscal year our wages increase, it is because we have all demonstrated a performance that is satisfactory. When our health benefits expand, it reflects our satisfactory performance. Satisfactory is what we are, what we shall be.

Nevertheless, we must meticulously assess the particular ways in which we are each, individually, satisfactory. We prepare for months in advance, I and my superiors, reviewing my performance plan from the previous year, determining which aspects have been met or not met, justifying the discrepancies, putting a modest check mark next to goals that have been met—to satisfaction, of course—tallying how many goals (of all the goals) one might reasonably expect me to have met, and then determining whether that standard of what is reasonable *has* been met. If it has, we advance the argument that therefore, my performance as a whole, evaluates to the ultimate annual *satisfactory*. That single measure of my effectiveness as a valuable member of the organization.

The meeting is at nine am.

There are no meetings scheduled before nine am. We wouldn't want to leave out anyone who logs in at eight thirty. And someone might be late. If someone were late, we wouldn't want to assume that it weren't for some good reason. We don't carry on without our colleagues, for to do so would be to blame them, to cause them to miss out, when it is well known amongst everyone and formalized as a prefacing statement in the employee handbook that *situations do in fact occur*. We don't encourage distrust amongst our colleagues, whose motives are, we must assume, only ever good, and whose tardiness is always due to a justifiable circumstance, for which the organization should certainly provide accommodation— or better yet, avoid the situation entirely, by scheduling meetings a safe distance away from everyone's presumed arrivals, i.e., some time after those of us who come in late arrive.

At exactly eight thirty, nine if we were late.

I look at my inbox and attempt to calculate, based on the names alone, how long it will take to answer each email. I do not open any, as I do not want them to mark them as Read. As long as I have emails to respond to, I'm busy. I am always busy. I will always be busy, and in order to make sure I keep on being busy, I calculate the time it will take to write my anticipated answers to the sorts of inquiries these people send —though not all of them are known—and I balance that against the organization's forty-eight-hour response policy. For every email merits a response, even if there is no answer to the question at hand. I should say, rather, that there's a reply rather than a response. But there are also always contingencies. If there are simply too many inquiries to which to respond, we've been known to set an auto-response on the inbox to warn the inquirers that their replies may indeed take longer than the forty-eight-hour service standard, and by setting that auto-response, we have technically responded to the email in time—in very good time, in fact. Immediately.

At nine am, my boss will start the meeting, as it is within her duties to open the meetings. In advance of the meeting, we have worked out exactly how I am good and what I shall require to thrive in the coming year. I can't be expected to thrive without the proper equipment and resources. It was difficult, this year, coming up with something I still lack in order to fully thrive, but ultimately, we settled on an audio headset, which should optimize my video communications with both internal and external stakeholders. But let's not get ahead of ourselves; this all still needs to be worked out.

My boss and I have an understanding and, I think, some mutual goodwill. Prior to our entrances into the organization, we both worked in much more high demand positions, for lower compensation. We both sacrificed for the sake of our employer, and we both suffered because of it. We both enjoy both cats and cat pictures, and I let her know whenever Dorian's done something exceedingly adorable. We both allow ourselves the luxury of a walk away from the desk now and again. Now there is the matter of my ongoing inferiority, which remains assured, so long as she remains in a higher position than mine, with extra responsibilities besides. We differ in that she chose to have a family, whereas for me, it's not quite right. And you know people always question how worthy of a human you are, if your house isn't always full of other humans whose needs you must attend to, but it is right for me, and in fact, the best decision I've probably made, along with quitting that old job and coming to the organization.

As she appears on my screen, my boss' expression indicates that it is time for business alone. For the purpose of the evaluation, she has adopted the inscrutable face of a superior. Our interactions today will be purely transactional, although I know, precisely because of this demeanor she has adopted, that our implicit pact remains. We both have roles to play, and there is a game here to win. Other faces appear, older and more superior to Sonya, faces I see perhaps once or twice a year, but whose edicts are nevertheless always apparent in my own work and methods. They are the embodiment of the organization, and I am but one of its fingers, working alongside and in tandem with the others, to accomplish a purpose that was thought of far away from any of us, impulses from the more nearby musculature controlled by a will that's enacted through these many parts and their collaborative labour. Though from my particular point of view, it's unclear how what I do at any moment is contributing to their strategies and plans. Nevertheless, if it weren't so, I likely wouldn't be around. The meeting starts within a minute of its schedule, in order not to let the clock advance to the next minute.

"My name is Sonya Patronov, and this is the annual evaluation of employee Clarissa Knowles."

The upper ups start turning off their cameras, now that the meeting is underway. They express, sometimes, that they don't want to interfere with the proceedings, only observe, and it's implied that if they're not paying attention, it's because they're working on something on another screen, something very important, something that *cannot* be questioned. I suspect, but would absolutely neither hint nor aim to demonstrate, that none of that is occurring.

"The employee's tasks pertain to the ongoing administration of the program. The employee's contributions to the administration of the program have been invaluable."

I watch my face on the miniature preview, keeping it neutral. This is not the time to have any defining qualities.

"The employee, as a regular part of her duties, must, in addition to administering the program, respond to inquiries about the administration of the program." Indeed, my responses must be limited in such a fashion; otherwise, it might be implied that I were doing something other than administering, that there might be some way I'd intervened in the trajectory of the program, or that I had otherwise influenced the results of the program, where such influences were completely inappropriate for a 07.

"The employee has, in addition to her functions, completed ten courses offered by the organization's internal school of learning. I will share my screen to enter the document into the video record."

Of course, the meeting is being recorded. We must keep very careful track of everything that occurs, in case of an audit. Who might perform the audits—that's not clear. Everyone is always so very busy, it's not clear who among us might decide to go back and review the meeting, analyze the document, and calculate how much time I had spent on mandatory training courses: Civility; Respect; Communication; Integrity; Security, and so on, the values of the organization listed in front of us, my certificates of completion evidence of to what extent I embodied those values, to what extent I had *become* the organization.

"Now you see evidence of the employee's competence with regard to external queries. On my screen is an email response from the Associate Vice President of Finance at the University of Northern South East. I will read the response aloud for those who would benefit from an aural representation of its content. The email says, 'Thank you, Clarissa, for your quick and thorough response. That does indeed answer my inquiry.'"

It was always nice of the institutional administrators to send those responses; most of the institutions I work with don't bother. Once they've got the information they want, they're off, not to be heard from again until they want something else from me, some other hint of how to best to qualify for the funding that our program offers through the organization, never thinking to wonder if maybe, if they were kind enough to send just a brief note in appreciation of the service I provide, I might be of some additional assistance, despite how I am mandated not to be. But to them, I'm nothing more than a policy link on a screen. It takes some insight to recognize that some policy links are more helpful than others.

"Before I conclude the evaluation, I would ask the employee to report on her subjective experience of her employment within the organization. Clarissa, do you agree with the evaluation as heretofore discussed?"

Using my given name only to indicate that the organization cares about me much in the way someone would who uses my first name.

"Yes, I agree."

"Please note that it is the organization's policy to provide reasonable accommodation for any illness or injury that could demand such accommodation, should the employee feel that such accommodation would assist in the completion of the employee's tasks, regardless of whether the illness or injury is documented by a medical professional, and where such illness or injury may be either mental or physical. Does the employee require any accommodations going forward?"

"No."

"Does the employee have any suggestions for how the organization might better support the employee in the employee's ongoing career and other goals?"

The generic question was meant for all employees, and where a question is meant for all employees, it's best not to use any pronouns at all; thus my boss became very good at repeating the phrase, "the employee" without it seeming unfit for a human mouth to utter ad nauseum. And if I were being honest about my goals, I'd say that were one of them. But instead, I promised to make a modest suggestion, correlated to an anticipated modest improvement in performance, for a modest cost to the organization, to be returned in multiple through increased productivity. If all happened according to my and Sonya's plan, what seemed like an inconsequential expense would, over the course of the bureaucracy, become standardized to all 07 employees, becoming a great expense and a vast alteration to the way things are done. I must introduce the idea here as if that is not the case, as if this particular decision to grant mere hundreds of dollars will not inevitably alter the equipment orders for every new employee ongoing and thus the organization's technology budget for the foreseeable future. But Sonya knows that, and this is why we're doing this.

"The organization," I said, as we had practiced, "has always kept abreast of technological advancements and the capacity for those advancements to contribute to the efficiency and efficacy of its employees. I suggest that, to optimize my performance, the organization agree to purchase a headset, in anticipation of a time when queries are best answered live over a video stream."

Like fireworks lighting up the night sky on the anniversary of our president's birth, faces began to appear on the screen. For the suggestion was not so modest after all and, as we had anticipated, the suggestion that the purchase of headsets (currently limited to positions of a level 09 or above) came off rather impertinent. But the higher-level administrators quickly regained their composure as they processed what I had said—that they were technologically advanced, that they had foresight, that workflows could be improved, and that they could be responsible for that improvement—and they quickly talked over one another to make it clear that they would agree to the modest cost, if only the record would show how quickly each one was to agree.

Something I worried about but had never flagged to Sonya was the possibility that the *office people* might someday want headsets too, or whatever device it was that would help that species to better communicate. Or if not that, some other performance enhancing device of equal value. But let that arise as an issue further down the line—it is impossible to speculate on how best to accommodate the employees whose physical forms may well have significantly changed since we'd last seen them.

Sonya acknowledged the success of our arrangement, looking directly at me through the screen. The matter was concluded: "The employee will report on the improvement to workflow at her next evaluation."

I nodded.

"Taking into account the employee's completion of the mandatory training, the employee's excellent performance in administering the program, and the employee's excellence in responding to inquiries, I conclude that the employee's overall performance during the previous fiscal year might be reasonably deemed"—she paused, as if she were calculating the results of her evaluation at this very moment—"satisfactory."

"The meeting is concluded."

Without any further discussion, the screen went black. With the image still fresh of my boss' face on the screen, the headset lending its constant air of authority to her words, her face, her being, I saw my own face reflected back on the blank screen, and I imagined that same headset placed upon it. With it, I would come ever closer to embodying the role of employee of the organization, with its attendant rights and responsibilities. The headset would communicate on my behalf how important my communications were. The institutions would appreciate and learn to love me. The organization would continue its operations without deviation—the highest praise the organization has to offer.

Maurice would have loved to see it all play out. *You don't even want the headset*, he'd say. *Even your desires are theirs.*

No, Maurice, I'd tell him, *they're mine now.*

3

When I exited the program, I saw a message from Syeda: "I'm dying to know how the evaluation went."

Syeda is my best friend at the organization. She's always dying to know how everything is going. When I first started at the organization, she set up a meeting with me, to welcome me. I thought it was something official, the whole team, getting to know me. But it was just Syeda, there on the screen, and me dressed my best, thinking this was how people were going to know me from now on. And she kept doing it. At least once a week, she'd add a meeting to my schedule. We could all see when one another was free, so she knew when would be best. I couldn't make an excuse. Once, after a few months, I asked her if she met with everyone this way. She said of course not; she'd be in meetings all day. She said that she only did this with me, because she wanted to have a work friend. She said that the way to make a friend was to choose someone with whom you'd get along, and then to meet with them regularly.

She wasn't wrong.

More importantly, I liked her. Syeda was everything Maurice thought impossible about working for the organization. She went about her tasks with a sense of individuality that meant people often thought they were being treated contrary to protocol, that they were being given some special benefit thanks to Syeda's intervention, when in fact, she dealt with everyone the same as the rest of us did—except with personality. Syeda's way of dealing with the world meant that you could be an individual and *also* one of many. It wasn't a choice that had to be made, *Maurice*.

At the same time, if Syeda had her way, she'd ruin annual evaluations for everyone. She was always hoping to be better than satisfactory. I think she might even have been happy with *anyone* being more than satisfactory. Surely someone had to be "good." Is there no good in this world? Do we not have any control over what others believe about us? If there's no difference between me and the next person, who am I?

The answer is: a well-paid employee of the organization. Syeda didn't seem to connect the dots between how we're all both excellent and satisfactory and how we all deserve exactly the same pay and benefits. But that's the end goal of it all— equal pay for equal work. We must have *equal pay* for *equal work*, but Syeda would argue that *no*, because the *work is not equal*, neither might be the pay! She thought perhaps if someone did more, they might *get more*. Surely there's such a thing as meriting *more*, but *actually no there isn't*. It's what Sonya and I had come to realize before we got here—more work will get you nothing more in terms of remuneration. More work gets you more work, for the same pay. Then the people who don't work more get less, because they're not doing the standard more, because yesterday's more is today's "satisfactory."

There's no way to outrun it. The overachievers of today become the satisfactory of tomorrow.

It is best to avoid that.

Syeda reminded me of one of my roommates, back when I was studying as an undergraduate. Lauren used to leave little notes around the house, asking everyone to please just be a little bit better. She'd be so nice about it. "Hey guys, can we please not leave open metal cans in the fridge?? They release toxins. :-) :-) Thx!!!" Lauren always had a point to prove. If she wasn't writing it out on the whiteboard, we'd still get the message. She would find a way to let everyone know what her stance was. Like when she started leaving her Diva cup on the bathroom counter. We all knew she was making a feminist point about the beauty of a woman's reproductive cycle and about how we had all been socially conditioned to react with disgust to something perfectly natural, and she was just waiting for one of us to have that reaction around the house. But of course none of us would, because we all knew that the point she was making was that we *shouldn't*, so we couldn't. There it stayed, those many months. Meanwhile, I kept wrapping my tampons in toilet paper before putting them in the trash, like some tool of the patriarchy.

I imagined that Lauren grew up to be Syeda, and now it's like we've known each other forever. It's how I dealt with the general truth that people will come and go from my life, that the window in which I know them is too small to infer much beyond, and that when you don't know someone to the extent that I don't know anyone, we are all ultimately alone. I pressed "Chat" on the screen.

"How'd it go?" Syeda wanted to know.

"Good morning!" I said.

"Yes, good morning! How did it go?"

"I got Excellent. They're giving me a raise. They told me not to tell anyone."

"Bullshit," she said, but her eyes worried at me. I let them for a moment.

"I'm excellent in every way, and that earned me a solid satisfactory."

Her eyes settled down again, assured that I hadn't outdone her. Now she could be a supportive friend again.

"I told you the system was rigged. If it were up to me, you'd be running this place. You're so much smarter than those assholes."

"I don't want to run this place. That sounds like work."

"Just what do you think they're doing all day with their cameras off?"

I thought back to about six months ago, when a level 09 accidentally left her camera on when she joined our meeting. There she was, facing off to the right. She had a butter knife in one hand, bread in the other. What could she have been doing?

I surely wasn't aiming at a promotion without knowing that.

"I don't even want to know."

"You're so frustrating, you know that."

"Shhhh. I have a reputation of being satisfactory to live up to."

"Ha ha ha," Syeda said.

She saw a look on my face as I opened my email on another screen.

"What's going on?" she asked. "Why does your face look like that?"

"It's an email," I said. "I don't know this person."

"Tell them to fuck off, then." We laughed.

"I'm not exactly sure what they want."

"I'm always available for a consult."

That was one of the main ways the level 07's kept busy—we consulted with each other about how to answer the inquiries. That's why some of the inquiries took so long to answer. We have to make sure everyone is *on the same page*. One of the organization's greatest fears is that one of us will cite a policy that appears or is contradictory to a policy cited by another employee, and that someone will make the explicit comparison, such that they end up looking like fools. Our efforts to avoid that situation translates into a series of activities that can't possibly be tracked using productivity software. That's where most of the day went, if anyone asked how we were all so busy. Making sure everyone is on the same page is what's keeping us all in business.

"OK, thanks."

In her customary fashion, Syeda wasn't interested any longer, now that she knew I hadn't outdone her in any way. She disappeared from the screen, and I stared in wonder at the email, the words not making any sense from within this context. Was it a real proposal? Something an applicant was mistakenly sending through email instead of through the online portal? Was it a tech support issue, that I could forward along with the message that I was forwarding it along, and thus meeting the requirement of responding while delegating the actual response to someone else? Was it an accident, something meant for someone else, not actually meant for us at all? That would explain why it seemed so out of sync with the rest of my correspondence.

What is it this guy wants from me?

It was sent at 11:32pm from Dick Richards, Associate Professor of Humanities at East South Western University.

The email says, "I propOSE we fill those HOLES, babyyyyyyyyyyyyy."

It didn't seem right. The formatting alone was out of sorts. The organization is so strict with its formatting require-ments for queries, I wasn't sure if this deviant capitalization and letter repetition would even allow me to count it as a query. But it was in 12-point black Arial font, which is how I suppose it got past the initial administrative review.

As for its content—was he implying that the program's goal of filling gaps in the organization's funding initiatives (identified by the annual survey of funding recipients) was not being met?

Indeed, it would require a consult, but I thought better of asking Syeda, who might just have a brilliant response, and thus prove that there was someone better than satisfactory among us. I would ask the team as a whole—at least, those of us who had moved to the units. It was the organization's stance that the individuals working from the office had "devel-oped an alternate expertise" that rendered their opinions on our day-to-day work irrelevant.

I entered the community room.

"Team, I need a consult."

Emily was there, so was Melissa, Shabtai, and Henri. We'd lost Mia to the office. Good riddance, I thought. She never heart-reacted to the photos I shared of Dorian, and the lack of reaction emojis implied an attitude of superiority—she thought that either my concerns were frivolous, or she was trying to indicate that she couldn't dedicate any time whatever to building team morale, her own pursuits being so much more important. I hope Mia has six toes on each hand by now, but chances are I'll never know.

I shared my screen. There it was again. "I propOSE we fill those HOLES, babyyyyyyyyyyyyy." I felt like the message became more powerful, the more screens on which it appeared, but also, the responsibility for it diffused, so that when I eventually did respond to it, the response would not be *mine*, but *ours*, the force of an entire department behind the few sentences it would merit.

"How did this make it past the 02's?" Henri wanted to know.

"I don't know, but it was assigned to me."

Emily: "What are the 02's going to do, delete it?"

"Exactly," I said. "Every email must be answered in forty-eight hours."

Melissa: "What do you say to that, though?"

Me: "Is there a policy?"

Melissa: "We don't have a policy on this."

Me: "Can I pretend I didn't get it?"

Henri: "Not once it's assigned."

I quit sharing my screen. They'd seen enough.

Emily: "The system would have already generated a receipt for it, if it's assigned."

Well fuck, I wanted to say, but you can't say that in the community room.

"You're going to have to send something in response."

"Pretend he asked something else," Henri said. "Just answer some other question he might have asked, and no one will ever notice."

"What did you just say?"

Oh my god. I had my eyes on the other screen, and I didn't see her come in. It was McKenzie.

Sonya's boss. She was silent in the meeting this morning. Silence was McKenzie's currency of praise. Hearing her speak was a bad sign. A written pronouncement was even worse.

"Did you just tell a 07 not to answer someone's inquiry, Henri?"

"It's a special situation—"

"We're made for special situations."

I jumped in: "McKenzie, I don't think there's a policy for this."

"Then make one," she said.

Oh, thank goodness! Then no one will have to answer another one of these emails again! I thought. But I shouldn't have thought that, turns out.

"Does the inquiry express an unmet need of the research community?" McKenzie wanted to know.

"Well, I suppose so, in a way," I said.

"And does the program have the means to address the expressed need?"

"I suppose, technically, but it would mean going above and beyond…"

"Our team was specifically formed to meet the unmet needs of the research community by going above and beyond. Make it work, Clarissa."

And she disappeared.

One by one, they all left.

I was alone again, singularly responsible for answering the query, as every one of them abandoned me in the community room, McKenzie too returning to something much more important than 07-level queries. I looked at Dorian, on the chair next to me, reserved for visitors, even though there were never any. I patted him on the head, telepathically sending him the message that he should step on the delete key as many times as necessary, to provide a plausible excuse for why the query should go unanswered. The organization can't track human-cat telepathy, as far as I know.

"Just like people to disappear as soon as you need them, eh, Dorian?"

I still had almost thirty-five hours to come up with something. Certainly, a person with my background and qualifications, my knowledge of the program and its intricacies, would be able to come up with something. "It's a good thing we don't expect cats to know everything," I told Dorian. I would not—I refused—to think about it outside of working hours. I walked down the hall for a Diet Coke.

Dick Richards would have to wait.

4

I LOGGED IN AT EIGHT THIRTY AM. THE 02'S HAVE ALREADY been online for hours. There's a new message in my assignments from Dick Richards. It says, "Dear Clarissa Knowles, Please ignore my previous message. It was sent in error, to the wrong recipient, with the wrong words. I do not want you to respond to either that message or this message. I have already cleared the email policy deviation with Sonya and McKenzie. Thank you for your hard work on this endeavor."

BUT THAT'S NOT what happened, is it. It was just an imagining from that time just before awakening, when I tended to solve all of the day's problems in advance, only to find that when I actually awoke, the work hadn't stuck. The tasks were still to be done.

I fed Dorian, told him he was a very good cat, and logged into the system.

An actual message read, "I need you to update the list of members to include their phone numbers." It was from Devin Brault.

Devin was hired as an assistant last month, but if you ask him, it's been three or four months, *at least*. He showed up to our first meeting in one of those hundred-dollar t-shirts with some stupid logo on it that he didn't know how to take care of. Once he figured out how to turn his camera on, you could see the neck was all stretched out, and he hadn't fixed his hair. He said he'd spent the last decade as a "manager," but if you looked him up in the organization's open directory, you could find out he was really a *kitchen manager*.

"I managed a fucking medical practice before I got hired," Syeda said to me in the side chat as Sonya announced his hire. "I worked for the fucking UN."

And we all have to be careful about what we say to Devin Brault. At the drop of a hat, he'll be in HR to complain. At the same time, he thinks he should be running things. He's a level 02, but you'd never know it, based on his demeanor and how often he decides to tell the rest of us what to do.

When responding to Devin, it's very important never to speak to him directly. Wherever possible, we're advised to cite existing policy or, better yet, respond with a link to the same policy, and who knows, he might one day actually read something about how to do his job. So when I read that message, I spent an hour composing my response.

Greetings Devin,
Pursuant to your request to update member phone records, I refer you to our internal policy on the division of duties amongst staff: [INSERT LINK HERE].
The policy states that 02's "are responsible for maintaining and updating member records."
Please address questions to level 09.
Best,
Clarissa Knowles

A response came quickly after: "Haha, ok. I just thought it would be easier for you to do it. Thanks!"

Fucking wanker.

And there was still the matter of Dick Richards.

Before answering his inquiry, I looked him up in the database. Dick Richards was funded two hundred thousand dollars for a project on how artificial intelligence would combat the threat of artificial intelligence. He proposed that we should focus our human efforts on becoming more likable to some of the artificial intelligences likely to arise over the next few years—discover their tastes and adapt accordingly. The actual struggle for world domination would take place amongst them, and it was hubris to think that humanity would have any say in it. Our best hope was to change—to determine a role we might fill in the new society and to begin practice of that new role immediately, such that the new leadership would treat us benevolently as it reigned. Dick Richards proposed that manual dexterity would be valued in the coming civilization, and he recommended distributing stress balls to underprivileged communities.

I deepened my search. I found Dick Richards living in a house in the historical section of town, sold five years ago (to him) for a price beyond the means of a university professor. He had generational wealth—or *his spouse* did. Or his spouse made way more money than he did, if they exist at all. Where were they?

I didn't want to do it, but I got out my personal phone at work and searched social media.

Dick Richards didn't have a spouse in any pictures. He didn't advertise his relationship status at all. There were a few public posts about papers he'd published, conferences he'd attended, and of course that he'd been granted two hundred thousand dollars to anticipate the future of humanity, but there was nothing personal at all.

Dick Richards, though, was *hot.*

Sorry, Doctor Professor Richards.

Is hot.

Does Dr. Prof. D. Richards work out?

I prefer to think that he's got some other kind of activity going on to keep fit. Something not so explicitly vain. Like maybe his parents live on a farm outside of town, and on weekends he goes to throw hay bales around, and doing it every weekend makes his shoulders that wide, so his shirts look a little tight. Or maybe he's just at home reading, when he's got to stop and work out an idea in his head, and the only way to do it is through push-ups. Or maybe it's from throwing women around in bed, and that's how he got so confident as to send that inquiry. Perhaps it wasn't the only query he sent; he sent many of them, so many of them, he didn't need to throw hay bales that weekend, his arms were already sore from sending inquiries to women at the organization and beyond.

No, that can't be true, I reasoned.

It can't be true, because Dick Richards was hot enough that the thought made me a little jealous.

What if someone else had already answered his inquiry?

No. If he had sent more than one, they'd all be rerouted to me. Once an inquiry is assigned, all follow-up inquiries from the same email address are assigned to the same officer.

At least, within the organization.

But what if he was getting funding somewhere else?

I thought to what McKenzie had said as I composed my official response.

Greetings Dr. Richards,

Thank you for contacting the program with your inquiry. Your contributions to research are acknowledged and appreciated.
I have discussed your inquiry with upper administration, and we have concluded that your request is within the scope of the eligibility criteria of the program. Resources are available to you. As always, any resources provided by the program directly do not reduce your current funding.
The program is designed to support non-traditional research methods for the betterment of society. We strive to meet the unmet needs of the research community by offering flexible support to the researchers of the future.

Cordially,

Clarissa Knowles, Ph.D.

I leaned back and stared into the farthest corner, as my optometrist had recommended, to prevent eye strain.

But then McKenzie just invited me to a meeting—in two minutes.

What the hell?

She's calling.

What if I'd gone out?

I laughed.

I clicked on her call.

"Hello, Clarissa."

"Good morning, McKenzie."

We'd both attended the seminar on the importance exchanging greetings before revealing our true intentions, to make our interlocutors feel more comfortable.

"How would you rate your current workload?"

"Medium," I responded.

"And how's your mental health?"

"Very good."

"Oh!" she said. "I'm not used to hearing that. That's good. That's very good."

"Yes, I'm very good."

"I have a task for you."

"Sure thing."

"I need you to update the list of members to include their phone numbers."

A second passed.

"Clarissa?"

"McKenzie, I would like to understand the assignment of this task. I am a level 07, while the task is appropriate to a level 02."

"Clarissa, I know that the task is appropriate to a level 02; I was on the committee that wrote the guidebook of tasks and their assignments. But I really need your help on this."

We're trained to begin a sentence with the name of the person we're addressing. It indicates that we are thinking of them as a person and not merely in terms of the role they play within the organization. These recognitions of an employee's individuality will increase the employee's feelings of well-being and therefore productivity.

"I need you to say it."

McKenzie paused.

"*Devin's just not up to speed quite yet,*" I said. "Say it."

"Devin's just not up to speed quite yet," she confirmed.

Confirming that is necessary to later argue that I am performing the task on behalf of a colleague whose potential is not being fully utilized by the executives. Of course, they wouldn't want to say so. But somebody's got to take responsibility for the deviation. Still, it's not right. Devin was offered the appropriate training courses for the tasks to be assigned at his level. It's not really that he's not up to speed. Would he really rather people believe he's stupid than do work?

No. Because he doesn't believe that anyone would actually believe he's stupid. He'll go "home" during his off hours and brag about how he gamed the system to make a level 07 do his work for him. And he'll think that makes him smarter than I am.

"I might require overtime for this task."

I wouldn't.

"Whatever you need."

That's *thank you* in McKenzie-speak.

We're all affected by the Devin problem. McKenzie too. In the last few moments of our meeting, we exchanged looks of concern and despair, about the current issue as well as what it foretold, looks that would never be recognized by the organization's tracking software—for human eyes only.

5

"You'd better not be doing that asshole's work for him."

Syeda stared at my headset through the screen. It had arrived by courier this morning, and I'd already spent a half-hour unpacking it, reading the manual, and updating the employee equipment inventory.

Then I called Syeda, to tell her that the whole plan had gone off without a hitch.

Then I accidentally said, "These phone calls won't be nearly as tedious."

And she had asked, "What phone calls?" And I told her.

Then she said, "You'd better not be doing that asshole's work for him."

But I was doing that asshole's work for him. McKenzie had asked. She already told Sonya I was doing it. We were already short staffed because of all of our colleagues who had been reassigned work more appropriate to the collaborative environment at the office building. We all knew that was a cover-up, but *for what* was a matter for speculation. Nevertheless, we couldn't fill those positions unless they were vacant, and they were not. My colleagues who made it their business to care the most were preparing to argue that the reassignment of duties should result in the office people having a separate job classification that would render our positions vacant, but the committee was still being formed to handle any such policy clarifications as regarded the office people.

Sonya didn't assign me any new 07 work for the week, because I was already on assignment. I knew Syeda didn't mean to imply that she was angry with me, in particular—it's the organization that's to blame, and also Devin—but that's how I heard it, such that now I didn't know what to say. My headset started to feel out of place on my head, too tight and confining for the psyche.

Syeda went on. "That's how it starts. He'll take one of us down, and then the rest, until suddenly, we're all just here to execute his stupid ideas, and the organization falls."

"The organization won't fall; there are safeguards."

"You know what I mean."

I knew what she meant. The danger was that the organization would become something that it wasn't. For Syeda, that meant its mission would significantly alter, changing the course of our work, until she ended up working to support something against her own values—*traditional research*. For me, the danger is that the organization would restructure its workload, forcing me into tasks extending beyond my range of available hours—tasks that served no purpose at all and which would make my eight-hour days tedious. Tedious like these phone calls. *It had already begun.* The worst part was that I could feel the beginning of the slippery slope Syeda was afraid of, and that I indeed had something to do with it. When the organization "fell," all the good people would look back and pin the exact moment its destruction began at the time at which I agreed to perform a task that Devin Brault was not up to speed enough to complete. *And from there, it all went downhill...* they'd say.

"I've got to go," I told Syeda and left. I couldn't handle this level of responsibility, not all at once, not when it was all already basically done.

Not when I'd already doomed us all.

I looked at the list of members to call. Three hundred and sixty-six of them.

Best get started.

The organization predicted that each phone call, with the update to the member details, and the logging of the call in our expense database, would take five minutes. That converted to twelve calls per hour for thirty and one-half hours. It would take almost a week to complete the task—and it would take that long, no matter what. It is important that the organization demonstrate the superlative capacity to estimate the human resources required to any task.

My own weakness was always that I always had to make things more efficient, optimize them, do them *faster*. Such tendencies weren't welcome here, and for good reason. If I found a more efficient way of doing things, so would everyone else have to complete their tasks more quickly. The amount of available work would not increase, but productivity would. We'd stop hiring. Unknown people who could have contributed to the organization's mission would never be hired; unforeseeable damage might occur. Those who remained would be working as fast as we could; we wouldn't be able to book appointments during the day anymore—there'd be too much work to do. Leaves might not rollover into following years. "We just can't afford the time, and it turns out you're not using it anyway," Devin Brault would say, suddenly in a position of power. He'd release a personal statement on the website and a carefully crafted post on the organization's approved forms of social media: *From Kitchen Manager to Executive: How Devin Brault Optimized Productivity for the Organization.*

No. We can't have any of that.

Once I'm done with these phone calls, I'm done. The union would have my back if McKenzie kept being difficult. If Devin Brault's not going to do his job, they should hire another 02. It makes good fiscal sense, much more sense than having a 07 doing 02 tasks. I had my whole argument worked out by the time the database opened through the secure server, where I could access the member files.

Alphabetical. It always works.

"Hello, Dr. Abbott. It's Clarissa Knowles, from the organization. I'm calling to confirm that this number is the correct number at which to reach you. Can you confirm verbally that you can be reached at this number? Please respond within one minute of when you cease to hear my voice."

And so on.

I wondered, as I always did, what Dr. Abbott's and the other members' opinions were of me. Did they think I was a good officer? Did they appreciate the fact that behind the script, I was a person, whose livelihood depended, as so many of ours do, on an ability to play a role? Did they understand why it was necessary I greet them so formally? Did they understand that they also had a role to play, complimentary to my own, and that their conformation to that role had a lot to do with the seamless process of implementing the organization's mandates and, indeed, toward the betterment of research and society?

Two hours later, I got a message from Sonya.

"How are the phone calls going?"

"They're proceeding at a rate of five minutes per. The work will be complete in approximately four and a half workdays."

In truth, the calls took about two and a half minutes per. In between calls, I entered the reporting data into the logs. If I was unable to reach a member, I would specify "Unable to reach" in the database. Then nothing would happen. Nobody would follow up, try to find a new number, contact the member through any other means. There was no further attempt to update the number, unless the member contacted us and requested a change. Once the information was entered, I'd stare at the clock, waiting for it to turn, until it was time to start the cycle again.

Sonya's next message revealed the reason for her inquiry: "The executives would probably like to see some increased productivity to offset the cost of your new equipment."

I understood what she meant. We had conspired the whole time to get me this headset, and I had to demonstrate it was worth it, so that very quickly, everyone else might get one too, after which they'd stop counting the productivity minutes, and we could relax back into a normal pace.

"I am confident that, after a period of accustomization, I could demonstrate an increased productivity," I wrote. The headset actually made my job a lot easier, not having to pick up and hold the phone next to my head, not having to perform the ergonomic exercises meant to offset that repetitive action. But how much easier, it was best to let Sonya tell me that.

"The executives would likely be content to observe a five percent bump in productivity after said period of accustomization."

So, four minutes and forty-five seconds per call.

"That's in line with my anticipated increase."

"As always, if there are any external factors that should prevent the productivity reports from demonstrating accurately your excellent capacities—"

"I'll notify my immediate supervisor, who will take steps to ensure that the reports reflect that external factors beyond the employee's control do not reflect negatively on the employee's performance."

"Good g—" She stopped herself. The look on her face. She had almost said, "Good girl." *No Sonya, we can't afford a slip up like that. Not when the world is already crumbling.* But she stopped herself in time, and I, for my part, wouldn't note any suspicions regarding the unuttered syllable.

"Good. I'll let you get back to your task. And I'll not be assigning any new inquiries to your email until it's complete."

Dick Richards.

"What about existing inquiries?"

"McKenzie already approved the overtime."

"Thank you. I'll return to my task."

"The organization recognizes and appreciates your dedication."

As long as the organization pays me, they can have it.

6

DICK RICHARDS HADN'T RESPONDED BY THE END OF THE DAY.

He must be travelling in another time zone. Emails from all over the world come in at all hours of the night. We just answer them in the morning, or the afternoon. Things don't have to move any faster than that.

If he were in another time zone, though, he wouldn't have proposed a physical encounter in his first message, right? He would know that it was impossible, and he wouldn't have proposed it, correct? He had to be at home.

Dick Richards didn't check his email every day, because he didn't believe in being beholden to machines, or to the increasing demands made on people because of the convenience of said machines. Just because someone *could* now send him a message at any time of day or night didn't mean he would have to answer it. Dick Richards might think less of me if he knew I was concerned about at what time a message might be sent; he would think my way of dealing with the world had already begun to conform to the illusive happiness of a technologically advanced society—the false application of the term "progress" to mean technological progress and not the more basic notion of progress as a significant movement towards the ultimate *in-and-for-itself*, which as we all well know is happiness—and he would think less of me for it.

Even so, I waited two hours after my end time to see.

The overtime was already approved.

In the meantime, I got to know Dick Richards on my own, through his public persona.

Dick Richards was hired through a job posting uploaded by East South Western University six years ago. The position to be filled was for a tenure-track Assistant Professor in Future Humanities with a 2/3 teaching load with the possibility of a course release for externally-funded research. The incumbent would be expected to perform departmental and university service. The area of specialization for which the university was hiring was "Artificial Intelligence," while the area of competence listed was, "Anticipatory Theory." The hiring process extended 63 days beyond the deadline for applications, when a notice of his appointment was uploaded to a jobs wiki by an anonymous contributor. That normally happens when the applicant wants everyone to know they're hired but not to appear like they're bragging (even though they're bragging), but of course Dick Richards wouldn't do that. I'm sure it was someone from the institution, or even some other lurker on the job appointments site.

Dick Richards' house on Milligan Lane had two bedrooms and one and one-half baths, a garage, central air, forced water heating, included all major appliances, and a 10x10 storage shed in a small backyard, according to the real estate listing. The linoleum floors in the kitchen would have had to be replaced by now; they were already peeling then. Dick Richards would of course replace them himself, rather than having someone else do it. It's not that he needed to save the money; it's that with all of his intellectual labour, it felt good to do something with his hands. The curtains on the windows in that listing were all floral and lace—not Dick Richards' style. The newer image of the exterior on Satellite Streetview showed that he had updated those to white cellular shades, which meant he didn't have any animals sharp enough to cut them. If he did have animals, they were likely confined to their own small living space within Dick Richards' larger one—a rabbit, a reptile, a fish? No, I decided. Dick

Richards wouldn't have any animals confined in his house. He wouldn't believe in it.

In fact, he'd be strongly against it.

We would have to have a talk about Dorian, when the time came.

Dick Richards had an aunt Linda from Shucksville who died fourteen years ago of pancreatic cancer after a long illness. Donations may be sent in lieu of flowers to the pancreatic cancer awareness foundation. She was predeceased by her sister, Donna, and will be remembered by her other sister, Gina—one of these two women would be Dick's mother. He appeared in the short list of Linda's nieces and nephews who would remember her fondly: Robert Richards (Lisa), Ray Richards (Janice), and Richard Richards (Anna).

Anna?

Why does Dick have an Anna?

I shut off the machines, though I knew they never really powered down, and thought my thoughts.

Anna anna anna anna anna anna anna...

7

I'M AT THE OLD OFFICE, DOWNTOWN, BEFORE WE BUILT THE units. It's evaluation week, when all of the members come in to evaluate applications to the program. They sit in a room and sift through the pile, picking out whatever projects focus on topics that would reflect best on the organization.

Dick Richards is here.

He shouldn't be here. We only ask researchers to become members after their funding term. And he shouldn't be in the old office, either. When Dick Richards comes, he'll come to the new office.

Everyone else is pretending it's fine. They let him look through the applications as if it wouldn't constitute a conflict of interest. They take his judgments seriously. They nod and agree and disagree and agree. They agree that some applications are good and some are bad, and they disagree on some others, and in the end they separate the applications into an "agree" pile and a "disagree" pile. They agree that the "agree" pile will be funded, even the applications they agreed were bad, because bad or not, they agreed to them. I want to tell them, no, we can't fund the bad ones. It'll make us look bad. They have to look through the piles again, separate them by good and bad, not by agree and disagree. They have to. But the meeting is over. It's time to move on to the next room, and besides, it's not my job to tell the members what to do.

It's not my job to tell the members what to do.

It's not my job to tell the members what to do.

Dick Richards waits for me in the meeting room, as everyone else shuffles on to the next room, the next pile, the next agreements. It's the first indication that he knows who I am.

"So, how did I do?"

"Your contributions are acknowledged and appreciated."

"But how did I do at making you come?"

Now his hand was up my skirt, and I wanted to tell him that he was getting ahead of himself, that he couldn't have made me come yet, because he'd just started trying. He was conceiving of things in the whole wrong order.

But it's not my job to tell the members what to do.

"Dick?"

"Yes?"

"Fuck me. Fuck me fuck me fuck me fuck me fuck me fuck me fuck me—"

TWELVE POUNDS of cat fell on my chest. It was Dorian. It was his standard method for waking me, as soon as he heard the coffee machine had started. He'd jump up on the headboard first, then accelerate himself into my chest from there at nine point eight metres per second squared, using potential energy converted to kinetic energy to make the most of his small size. Once he knew I was awake, he ran off ahead of me into the kitchen, to prepare for breakfast.

What did that dream mean?

Was Dick Richards thinking about me, sending messages through my dreams? Where was Anna? Did he mean to let me know Anna was gone, that they'd divorced shortly after the obituary, that he'd never loved her anyway?

No, that can't be right. My Dick would never marry someone he didn't love.

And then there are the bigger issues.

Why was I thinking of Dick Richards outside of work hours?

What if the union found out?

Once, when the team had to complete a very important task on a relatively tight timeline, Syeda had mentioned that she was having trouble sleeping, because when she slept, she'd dream that she was still doing the work—but when she awoke, none of it was done. It happened to me as well. At the time, Sonya had told her that, if the work had been done when she woke up, she could have claimed the overtime. And everyone laughed. But then Sonya got serious, and she told Syeda to stop it. "Nobody should be dreaming about this job. Just don't."

It was against policy.

Of course, the idea was that our mental health and well-being would decrease if we spent our off hours thinking about work, so the answer was *just don't*. But what if I couldn't help it?

Maybe I'll ask Emily (the union rep) about claiming overtime. Then at least the organization would be assured I was being properly compensated for my mental labour.

Once I had prepared my appearance, fed Dorian, and prepared myself psychologically to face the day, I logged in. I saw that already, sometime before eight thirty, there had been an altercation in the general room.

Devin had started the conversation: "I need everyone to upload their .pdf's to the backup server. Thanks!!"

Emily had been the first to respond: "My .pdf's are in the regular folder, where the procedures said they should be. Is there another procedure of which I'm unaware?" Emily still thought she had to contradict men through questions rather than direct and literal phrases.

Devin: "It's just that the regular folder has to be backed up on the backup server. So I need everyone who put their files in the regular folder to add them to the backup server as well."

Syeda wouldn't have any of it.

Syeda: "Devin, are you really asking all of us to go through the regular folder, find our own files, and move them to the backup server, when you could literally just copy the whole folder over yourself, in like, two clicks?"

Sonya, who was usually watching, but who also usually let us sort ourselves out without interfering, decided to jump in.

Sonya: "Devin, I think you can copy the whole folder onto the backup server. If you need assistance, the organization's self-guided tutorials on technical issues should help."

Devin: "Oh yeah, I guess I could. Haha. Thanks, that's what I'll do. Haha."

Fucking Devin, fucking numpty. I'm glad that was all sorted before I arrived; sometimes it's nice to be out of sync with my earlier colleagues. They can sort Devin out for the day before I have to. I have other problems to attend to.

Like, where the hell is Dick Richards?

There was nothing in the inbox.

Is Dick Richards dead?

You can't just trust people to be alive, day after day, after all.

It's so strange how much of our lives revolve around the people around us staying alive. Given how squishy the human body is, how prone it is to glitches, it seems an unreasonable standard to expect everyone we know to stay alive all the time. That's why, at the organization, we are all replaceable. There's always someone else who's doing the same thing as we do, who knows all the same things, who could step in and perform our tasks the moment it's confirmed we're dead. To me, the thought was incredibly freeing. It's so much pressure, trying to stay alive for everyone else's sake. What if I didn't want to? Now, thanks to the organization's built-in human resource redundancies, I could off myself anytime I chose, without having to worry about how anyone would get on without me.

What a luxury.

I made my calls to the members and, when it was time to take a break, I took a break. I resumed my calls, and when it was time to break for lunch, I broke for lunch. I resumed my calls, and when it was time to think about logging off, I stopped. Throughout the day, the woman who looked back at me from the faint reflection in the monitor screens—the one with the headset—assured me that even though a lesser human could perform this task, they could never do it *as well*. In between calls, I looked for more information about Dick

Richards (and Anna), but only small things, neat little bits of information that I could absorb between calls, without missing my four-minute and forty-five second timer that told me it was time to go again. Even so, I learned a lot.

Dick Richards was once featured in the local paper for being such a good sport supporting Anna's much more profitable career.

Anna is an executive for a well-known shipping company and has over five hundred connections on business people social media.

Dick and Anna were pictured together at a friend's birthday party four years ago, below which Dick had commented, "That was fun!"

But if you had to say so, was it really?

Dick was on the board of a scholarship program, along with fifteen other only semi-knowns, who together judged applicants based on their merit, persistence, value, and worth. Every year, one postsecondary student was awarded one thousand dollars paid directly to their tuition account—a piddling sum, given the big deal they made of it.

I'm sure Dick Richards didn't design the scholarship program, though. More than likely, he was roped into it by one of the other fifteen, who probably knew Anna, who wanted to make Dick feel better for not being a known among knowns, who gave him a pity spot on the board, who thought maybe, now that Dick was doing something worthwhile, someone would notice and offer him some more lucrative employment. *It's like Dick doesn't want to succeed*, he probably said when it didn't happen. *I'm not sure he's right for Anna…*

Of course. They would have broken up over it. Everyone would pretend to be friends once a year, when it was time to consider the *Barely A Real Scholarship* program's applicants, but then they would separate again, everyone saying the same thing: *Poor Dick didn't know what he had.* But Dick would go home, happy to have fulfilled the duty he swore he'd never perform again, happy not to be living a life with such fucked up priorities as Anna's friends had.

Home to the big house he still lived in, because…

Maybe he didn't?

Within Anna's circles, the less that was heard about it, the more you knew it was true. While I didn't read anything about Dick and Anna separating because of her underdeveloped sense of humanity, still there hasn't been anything about "Dick and Anna" in the past year, which does imply that there is no Dick and Anna. It's all very hush hush. But one day he shut the door and didn't come back. Anna threw herself into her work, taking a lover on the West coast, where she knew they'd never run into anyone from back home. As she gazed out over the water in the early mornings, she appreciated that the view from his beach house was never what she thought she had wanted; nevertheless, it was what she wanted all along, she was sure of it, in retrospect. She would always be the one in her social set who had lived a wild youth, who had married a poor professor, who probably had stories, if you were willing to put in the effort to really get to know her. She banked on that new mystique after the divorce, which became her new husband's leant mystique, the man who had tamed the wild woman. Anna recognized that, at this point in her life, she was living exactly the life her parents had always lain out for her, and that besides that, she was enjoying it. And she thought to herself, *That's how it is. You have to let tigers wear vertical stripes.*

Was any of it true?

I'd be able to see it in Dick Richards' demeanour, if it ever comes to that.

I was supposed to log off fifteen minutes ago, but then when I looked back at the inbox, I couldn't. It was Dick. Dick was there. Dick Richards had responded to my email. The email came direct, because the original query had already been assigned. If Dick was responding to me, did that really mean there was no more Anna?

Dick Richards had written, "Let's see these resources."

8

"ARE YOU AVAILABLE FOR A FACE-TO-FACE NOW?" I ASKED HIM through the email system, hoping he was still online, that my message wouldn't be as obsolete as my existence by the time it got to him. The video chatting software wouldn't record our every word—which is to say, I would turn off the setting that let it. At the organization, sometimes we would turn that off when we wanted to say something that shouldn't be written down. When there was information to express that couldn't be part of the organization's transcripts. Sonya and I always turned off the recording function—and it was our right as private citizens to do so, even if the interaction would be deemed an official work interaction. The organization does not believe that the individual gives up their privacy due to their need to support themselves financially—you can't take someone's rights away by making it a condition of the job.

The policy was a good one, and of course we took advantage.

I followed up the message with a link to my personal web room.

The setting was more appropriate for short meetings with research administrators at institutions to confirm or discon- firm rumours they had heard from other research administra- tors at other institutions about updates to the policies that might benefit them, and I barely had time to change the ambience of the background and the actual physical lighting of the room before this man appeared on the screen.

It was the man from the photos, but moving. As I perceived his body in motion, through the many angles it presented, as opposed to the one apparent in a static photograph, I noticed he seemed a little older now, a little wearier. Was it because Anna left? Did he still have the house on Milligan Lane? He had a background, and his microphone was muted, so I couldn't tell where he was or what he might sound like. It's so jarring when you hear someone's voice for the first time. At the same time, as soon as I do hear someone's voice, it's as if it's been theirs all along. Would Dick Richards say something, since I was the one who spoke last in the email? What sort of standoff would this turn out to be?

He didn't say anything, so as I usually would in a videoconference, I took lead.

"Thank you for attending. We understand that your time is valuable, and we acknowledge and appreciate your contributions."

Dick Richards tilted his head to the side and smiled. I waited for some compulsory response.

Then he put a finger to his lips.

I couldn't imagine a video chat where no one speaks.

The productivity software would go crazy. Even when the recording function was turned off, it would receive a report of how long the call lasted and *how much* (but not what) was said. It was the exact amount of privacy the organization could justify maintaining in balance with its values. I worried about how the organization would interpret a silent video, and assured myself that in the worst case scenario, I could say it was connected by accident. After all, it was already after hours. But then again, I was claiming the overtime, so this wouldn't work at all.

As I figured it all out, Dick Richards made a hand signal that I knew meant he wanted my shirt off, and I balked, because his email had indicated he was about something else.

That's not where the holes are, Dick.

Did he recall the terms of the program, or did he even read them? Syeda hated when the awardees didn't read the terms of the program. To be fair, I told her, they're over a thousand pages long. *Have you read them?* I had asked her. *My online hours don't allow for the completion of such a task in addition to my regular duties*, she had said.

Aha! I thought.

But it's different for them, when they're taking our money, she reasoned.

We always talked about it as "our money," even though we'd never see any of it. At the same time, we looked down on the smaller programs with smaller budgets. They're not funding projects to transform social society and the well-being of its people. They're paying grad students to drink in Europe for a month.

It doesn't matter now. I took off my shirt, as Dick asked, undoing the buttons and weaving it around my body to avoid the headset I thought I would need for this encounter. I knew my angles around this camera well; I paid attention to that. People always think you're a better person if you're attractive, so just be attractive. It's called light and angles.

I had the camera lifted up from the top of my desk, and I pushed it back. Then I leaned my arms on the desk and pushed them together, amplifying my breasts with my arms and pushing up cleavage from the lace bra I'd put up with all day just in case Dick Richards finally showed. I wanted him to like me.

He liked me.

I started to remove my headset, but Dick Richards shook his head.

No, leave it on, the move said.

I could see his right arm moving something out of shot, and then I gestured. *Do it on camera*, which he understood. I think when Dick Richards signed into this call, he thought he was the one in charge. And he probably was. But we as a society always underestimate how pathetic men look masturbating, and especially sitting in front of a laptop, directed at a screen, waiting for something to happen, something *I would have to do*, to let this all go on. But I liked Dick Richards, so I did.

I moved my camera back on the desk and angled the screen down a little. Then I pushed my office chair back a bit, locked the wheels in place, and put my knees up on the side of the desk. On screen, he could see my legs but not my feet, which were too far out of frame. I pulled up my skirt and showed him how close he was to getting to see my pussy, if it weren't for the underwear. I started touching myself through the panties, just playing, just to get him.

He turned his mic on, a sign of his newfound subservience.

"Please may I see the resources." His voice was higher than I'd expected, the pace of his syllables quicker than I'd imagined.

I responded, now that I was allowed to speak, "Of course."

I removed the underwear and put myself back in the chair, full frontal framed by an office skirt with all the wrong parts covered. With my fingers, I took him on a slow tutorial of my anatomy. I looked at how hard he was grabbing at his cock and provided a counterpoint by being slow and methodical. I slapped my clit a couple of times, and Dick moaned; he hadn't muted himself again. The recognition of sounds by our software would support the interpretation that this wasn't an accidental call—that the overtime was legitimate.

I realized I could make him say anything. But what was the fun in that?

I wanted to get off, but it would take a concerted effort, and I was worried I wouldn't come off as a lady. Luckily, Dick had an idea.

"Turn around," he told me.

Right. He wanted to see all the holes, as the original inquiry had specified.

I turned around on my chair, as gracefully as I could. My face pressed against its back; I put my knees up on the seat and lifted my skirt toward the camera. From there, Dick could see any of the holes he wanted. And I could rub my clit until I came, while he was focused on other things.

I've missed fucking, I realized, since Maurice. So much so that, turned around, I didn't care much what Dick Richards was doing back there. Would he be upset if I finished first? But none of those concerns would actually matter because, when I turned around, he was gone. Either he'd finished and turned me off like a porno that lost its lustre after the second cum shot, or he had connectivity issues. It didn't matter.

I had responded adequately to an inquiry addressed to the program, within the allotted time, and I was reasonably certain that the researcher was satisfied. As I rearranged my clothing and office furniture, I thought of Maurice. Sex was better with Maurice. It was physical, literally warmer, thanks to the exchange of body heat, and then we got to talk a little after, about the important things. Maurice always acted like he could do anything, be anything, and he wanted me to acknowledge that when he said he was going to do something, that it was possible or probable for him to accomplish. It was like he wanted the praise in advance—and for things I knew were, for me at least, actually impossible.

Goddamit, Maurice, I had told him, *not all of us get to imagine other lives.*

Back in the living section of my unit, I cried over him for the thousandth time.

9

WE LIVE AND WORK IN THE UNITS, AND THE OFFICE PEOPLE live and work in the office. It used to be that when it was time for the members to come evaluate applications, we would all go to the office and pretend like we worked there all the time. But otherwise, the software sufficed to allow us to communicate and to meet productivity standards.

We might never have figured that out, if the new office hadn't failed so catastrophically.

Oh god, that new office.

The new office was a terrible idea.

It always had been.

They didn't listen to us.

The executives wouldn't listen to anyone.

The idea of the new office seemed so novel, so futuristic. They were going to revolutionize the workspace. No one would have desks. There would be zones for independent work and other zones for collaborative work, zones for internal meetings, and zones for meeting with external stakeholders. We asked if the executives would have to work in the zones as well, but no one answered.

You get to know the meaning of silence. Silence is always the answer everyone assumes but doesn't want to be true.

In a building attached to the new office, accessible

through the main floor hallway, we'd have our units. In the underground corridor between the units and the office, there would be retail and other commercial space—an optometrist, a dentist, a courier and restaurants. Our internal surveys had shown that a significant factor negatively impacting workplace satisfaction was the commute. The old building was downtown; there was no parking, and the number of people coming in on public transit meant that not everyone could possibly arrive at once. That was how the notion of flexible hours actually started. We had to stagger arrival times so as not to overwhelm the light rail transit system.

The organization eliminated the commute by providing us with units furnished with beds and a small kitchen area. In the interest of equity over equality, the units were customizable to an individual's requested reasonable accommodations. Some of my colleagues resisted the units—for a while—because they thought that if they both lived and worked at the organization, they would become mere drones, never out of the organization's sight, always acting for its purposes and in its interest, nowhere to think for themselves.

They thought a unit would make them a *less than one*.

As we moved into our units and started working in the new office, issues quickly became apparent. Without assigned desks, we had to bring our equipment home at night. Some of my colleagues became attached to certain workspaces and started coming in earlier and earlier to make sure they could claim them. Tensions rose, and some individuals began sleeping in the office, like nerds in the overnight line at an electronics shop whenever a new video game system was released, except the only reward here was "the good corner."

The real problem, as we told the executives, was that the new office only had fifty percent of the space of the old office. But the executives assured us that the space was designed to encourage movement, and that movement would ensure that no one was ever in the space that anyone else would need—not at the same time.

They were wrong. Having no assigned space meant that no one moved; everyone became static, afraid to leave their preferred area for fear that the area might be conquered by another, who had as much claim to it as they did. The fifty percent of people who were always supposed to be in transit from one area to another didn't exist. The zones became crowded, everyone politely agreeing to share the space while staunchly maintaining a territorial boundary.

The first person I remember retreating to the units entirely was Amira. We walked into the new office together on the first day it opened, with our laptops in our matching carrying cases, the organization's logo emblazoned across our backs. The union had demanded the technology packs, once it figured out that we'd have to transport the 8-pound computers morning and night, to the office from home or the units in the morning, and back again. The technology packs were ergonomic.

On that first day, Amira and I walked through the automatic safety glass doors and looked around for a place to set up. The straps on my technology pack were digging into my shoulders, but I figured my body would become accustomed to it over time. Amira's expression turned quickly to despair when she realized there was no space set aside for employee belongings, including the meals we had packed for the afternoon, to avoid the extra cost of the restaurants. "Where am I supposed to put my lunch?" she asked. I didn't know. I didn't bring one. "I guess I'll go put it back in the fridge in my unit," she said, and that was the last I saw of her in the flesh. On the screen, from then on, she was always in a unit.

I kept going into the office, finding space where I could, going down to the first floor for food, trying to make *myself* into a unit as much as I could, transportable from place to place, like the organization wanted. Self-sufficient, self-encapsulated, self-enclosed. I moved around and whenever I did, packed my things. I brought my workstation to lunch, to the bathrooms, to the basement retail outlets.

After about a hundred days, those of us who had moved into the units discovered that our out-of-office colleagues had been wrong about something. The danger of putting our units so close to the office wasn't that we would become drones for the organization. It was that the organization would become our home.

We infested it, like cockroaches with no concept of property law.

That is to say, we formed a well-ordered society, using the resources available to suit our purposes in order to optimize our living and working situations. With the executives a safe distance away, leaders emerged from among our set, whom we designated our "social coordinators"—an unpaid volunteer position with a time release from our normal functions. Nobody asked for the executives' approval. As they had told us, this space was *ours*, and we made it so. The first thing that had to be done was to provide reasonable accommodation to our anxious colleagues, who were already showing symptoms of a failure to thrive in the forced socialization environment imposed upon us. We sectioned off portions of the independent work zone and built barriers to enhance the illusion of distance. There were so many anxious people working for the organization, though, that the collaborative zones also had to be sectioned off.

As the space became reorganized in the manner to which we had become accustomed in the old office, less of it was available. At our morning meetings, the social coordinators would ask for volunteers to go work in their units that day. Then, to avoid having to ask every day, the social coordinators started asking for volunteers to go work in their units for the week. Every week, the same people volunteered and more, myself included, until finally, there was established a fixed subset of the workforce that remained in the office.

And they changed.

For a while, we could see from their backgrounds at the virtual meetings how the office was changing behind them. From the way they interacted, it was clear that there were new alliances, newly established social conventions. Jokes we didn't get. As long as the work continued, upper management did not concern themselves. But our colleagues were undergoing a transformation unprecedented within the organization. McKenzie, concerned for the organization's liability, once mentioned aloud the change to the proportions of their musculature. But rather than respond to the comment or request accommodation, the office people started taking our calls off camera. Their profile pictures replaced their online presence, the same ones we all had, with our shoulders angled forty-five degrees away from the camera, smiling straight on, the office hallway in the background. Within three months, they stopped meeting us, even audio only, their voices having noticeably risen and sharpened in the interim. Now evidence of their existence could only be gleaned by document version controls and the productivity software that continued to log their movements. The Committee for Health, Safety, and Accommodations speculated that the change was due to radon in the office building's air supply, which wasn't subject to the same building standards as the living quarters and therefore wasn't built to the same standard.

We have learned not to ask about them. We have retained our territory in the units and abandoned the office entirely. Although we might have expected to meet them in the tunnels, it seems they have elected to conduct their business there after hours—if they have any lingering business at all. It is no longer clear how the office folk live, nourish themselves, or what hierarchical system has arisen amongst them to ensure the continued functioning of the organization.

The office had always been a bad idea.

10

When I logged in at eight thirty the next morning, there was some discussion about how to answer an inquiry from an applicant whose funding application had been denied.

Or, as he wrote, "Why was my funding denied?" No signature.

After searching the email address, the team discovered that the email had come from Doug Newton, Assistant Professor of Chemistry at University of the East North.

To me, it was obvious from the way the email was worded: he was an entitled cunt. The fact that he referred to it as "my funding," as it if were already his, irked me. He never had to work for anything in his life, I imagined, based on that possessive adjective alone. I was immediately glad we didn't fund him, and secondarily curious why.

Looking into the particular application, Syeda discovered that Doug Newton hadn't actually proposed any project. The application was excluded for not having met the minimum requirement of being an application. Instead of a research proposal, Doug Newton wrote:

I'm very smart, and I'm sure I'll come up with something once the money is in hand. In fact, I probably shouldn't waste my effort on coming up

with something without the money, because my time is very valuable.
Once my funding application is approved, I'll let you know what my
project is, as long as doing so doesn't detract too much from my work.

Devin Brault was very impressed.

"It sounds like he's a very busy and important man," Devin wrote in the group chat. "I'm curious to find out why his application wasn't funded. Is it possible a 07 made an error inputting the approval of his application?"

Sonya clicked the button secretly removing Devin from the group chat. On his end, it would look like no one had responded, while we could continue discussing the matter rationally.

"Can I just write to him that it's because he's an asshole?" Henri wanted to know.

Sonya: "We'll have to find a nicer way of saying that." The mandate of the program requires we maintain collegial relations with researchers by treating them with respect. "Perhaps we can pull some language from the member reports."

The members, who were recruited precisely to examine the project's merits from all angles, evaluated Doug Newton's "application" and didn't have very nice things to say. In general, we would provide their comments to the applicant, so they could incorporate the feedback into next year's funding applications. But for Doug Newton, McKenzie had decided that we couldn't possibly pass along the member comments as they were written. They read:

Fuck this guy.
A waste of everyone's fucking time.
I didn't think we needed a criterion for douchebaggery in the rubric, but
apparently we do, thanks to Doug Newton.

When the reports were submitted, they were filed in Doug Newton's file, and his email notification of the failure of his application somehow didn't include the original reviewer reports. Technical issues do happen.

We thought he wouldn't have the gall to ask for them.

But here we are.

Sonya: "We need to take these and edit them into something that embodies the organization's commitment to respect while maintaining the essence of the members' comments."

Henri: "Clarissa, could you help with that?"

Sonya: "Clarissa, Henri is asking because there was a message in the inbox this morning from a researcher who was very impressed with your communication. It seems you were very helpful to Dick Richards, and he has some further questions. But first, could you clarify the members' comments for Doug Newton?"

Of course, I was more interested in what Dick Richards had to say, but I couldn't let on in front of Sonya and Henri. First, I would have to clarify the reviewer comments for Doug Newton. In the organization, the word "clarify" was used as a euphemism, whenever we had to correct a mistake, update something that was obsolete, or completely change our policies. Every change was labeled a clarification, and the façade that we never really altered anything in a meaningful way helped to assure everyone that the organization was a durable and resilient organization, founded on persisting principles, when in fact there were programs, policies, and people who had all been clarified out of existence.

They are never mentioned near the microphones.

I confirmed my new task. "I can clarify the members' comments for Doug Newton."

Sonya: "Thank you. The email is already assigned to Henri, so send him the clarification when it's ready."

"Absolutely."

As everyone disappeared to go about their business, I read the message from Dick Richards. It said, "Thank you very much, Clarissa Knowles, for your ASSistance! Do COME online again!!!" Sent at 12:42am.

I smiled.

Then I got a message from Devin Brault: "You did a great job with those calls. The member database seems up to date." How dare you say that to me, Devin Brault. *Your level 02 judgment is incapable of evaluating my 07 competence.*

A whole other distraction came through, from Syeda: "Did you hear there's an empty 08?"

She meant there was a position open at the 08 level. Sometimes it was because someone had left or had been clarified, but more often, it was because the organization had decided to expand its workforce. There was a bit of a competition between departments to see who could run the biggest program, measured by number of employees. So it was normal for the organization to be hiring.

"I didn't hear that. Are you going to apply?"

"Fuck yeah, I am. It's time."

Syeda had been a 07 not quite as long as I had been, but it was certainly long enough to apply for a level increase.

"You're great; I'm sure you'll get it," I told her.

"Aw, thanks. You weren't thinking of applying, were you?" She meant, *don't*.

"No, and as long as you're taking the position, you can pretend not to notice how long I've been a 07. I wouldn't want anyone expecting anything more from me. Deal?"

"You could easily get it too," she said, but only because she was assured that I wasn't competition. I reacted her message without typing words, a sign that I had work to do.

The thing was, it didn't matter what I said to Doug Newton. Of course, I wanted to tell him exactly what I thought—I wanted the member comments to be passed on without revision, and I imagined him, breaking down, realizing that his existence was meaningless, hating himself, cutting his wrists like an emotional teenager who wasn't invited out on Saturday night. But during my hours, I was playing the role of the organization. And the organization preferred not to think of individual circumstances. There were no exceptions to being respectful, because there weren't any particulars at all. The organization and everyone in it were the same and would approach every situation consistently and with the same level of civility, respect, and integrity. Even if the fuckers deserved none of it.

At first, I found this freeing—to think something else's thoughts, to use its words. My personal responsibility for what

I wrote was nothing, even though I would put my name on it —the researchers liked to believe they were communicating with an individual. But we all played the same role. It was a high school play, and we all had the same part, which meant we could run lines together, practice our modulation, and all the while assure ourselves that even though we were all playing the same role, we would certainly all put our own spin on it, just by virtue of being individuals. *You're not even thinking your thoughts*, Maurice would say. *Your personality is a procedures document.*

But that kind of thinking was for those of them who wanted to be individuals.

What about those of us who would prefer to disperse?

What if there wasn't any happiness to be found in holding together?

If only I didn't have to be somebody.

At least some of the time.

During the organization's time.

Oh god, what if I *were* an individual, a real and complex individual, who wasn't already fractured, and who had to do this?

Thank goodness, I'm not.

I wrote the following draft clarification of the members' comments about Doug Newton:

Another funding body maybe more appropriate to this project.
The time that the researcher intends to devote to the project could be more clearly stated in the proposal.
This project may inspire an innovative evaluation rubric for future competitions.

I sent the clarification to Henri and never heard anything of it again.

I responded to Dick Richards, suggesting I could respond to any further inquiries in my personal room the following evening.

PART TWO

11

I WAS ONLINE WITH DICK. I WAS WEARING MY HEADSET AND nothing else. I had my legs up around the camera, and I was penetrating myself with a flexible plastic cock that had arrived with the office mail, shaped to resemble Dick's dick. The package was still on the desk, torn open by its contraband contents, like my cunt was getting torn apart right now.

Dick was in the dark, his eyes shining at me on the screen.

Behind him I saw someone.

"Dick?" I said.

"Uhhhhhhhhhhhhhh," he started to come.

"Dick?" I said again, as she moved closer behind him.

"Uhhhhhhhhhhhhhhhhhhhhhh," he continued.

"Dick, she's going to find out about us."

"Uhhhhhhhhhhhhhhhhhhhhhh."

"Dick, she's right there. She's going to find out."

"Uhhhhhhhhhhhhhhhhhhhhh."

"Dick?" She put her hands around his neck and moved them up and down, like his throat was a giant cock, and she was giving it a two-fisted handjob. "Dick?"

"Uhhhhhhhhhhhhhhhhhhhhh."

She stared at me as he kept coming, as if to say she'd won. She'd won, because she touched him. She'd come in at the last second and stole Dick's orgasm out from under me. They were together, and I was alone.

They were alone together, Dick was coming, and my shotty plastic dick was cold and sticky.

> *This new person made it so I wasn't in any company at all.*
> *She came and took my Dick.*
> *"Anna, is that you?"*

I WOKE up too early for the alarm. Dorian was confused, but when I opened the can for his breakfast, he accepted it all the same, suspicious yellow eyes against grey fur, keeping an eye on me, to make sure I didn't try to take his early breakfast back. He would be upset when I didn't open a regular breakfast in another half hour, realizing finally that the early breakfast was all that he would get, and feeling very betrayed. I proceeded along my morning routine, noting along the way that I should figure out some method to make it take longer. I should have figured out how to shower longer, brush my teeth longer, clean Dorian's bowl for longer, so that I might not end up at my desk before eight thirty. But my own habits defied my intention, and there I was.

Eight fifteen.

I had a meeting with Sonya and McKenzie at nine. We had all checked in with one another multiple times, to make sure we were available, even though they dictated my schedule.

I knew why the dream bothered me so much—why I would have *that* dream. Why I would be bothered so much as to have it. Dick and I had been meeting after work twice or three times a week for four weeks. I still didn't know if Anna was in the picture or not. Surely, if she were, Dick would have mentioned her. Or he wouldn't have. At least to say to me that I shouldn't speak of our trysts to her. That they would have to remain clandestine.

But then again, he didn't talk much during our encounters. Sometimes, I had tried to ask him something, as soon as we'd gotten online, trying to get him to reveal something, to clarify something I already knew, or to catch him trying to deceive me. Between our meetings, I would formulate and reformulate the question I would ask next time, thinking on how best to word it, to force an answer from him.

Dick, I noticed your research has ethical implications. What do you think of the virtue of loyalty? Fidelity?

Dick, I see you have several graduate student trainees. Do you work closely with them?

Dick, I'm having trouble seeing you. Is there somewhere else you could go with a stronger signal?

Dick wouldn't answer. He would change the subject. Or more accurately, he wouldn't let me have my subject. Instead of responding, he would give me an order. Once last week, I refused to follow the order.

Show me how you rub those tittiiieeeeees, he'd typed into the chat.

I spoke into the microphone, to let him know I was serious. Like when at work, when we would call people on the phone if they didn't respond to a deadline on time. They wouldn't respond to emails; it was like they forgot we were human. So we would call them, let them know we had voices, that we were people, that we knew who they were, and that we expected things.

"Dick," I said. "I'd like to take this opportunity to remind you of my previous inquiry, and that I am yet to receive a response. Please answer me at your *earliest* opportunity."

When I said it, he turned around very quickly. His eyes turned off screen, and I saw him get up from his chair and disappear off camera, toward where he had been looking. I realized that there was no sound. He had muted himself before I'd said anything. Now he was closing a door, I figured. But the way he was doing it—

He was afraid.

It wasn't of me.

Was Anna outside the door?

Had he forgotten to close it?

Did she just return home, early, unexpected?

He appeared on the screen just long enough to press the End Call button.

Had it nothing to do with Anna?

Was it me? Had I overstepped?

I was so worried that Dick wouldn't show up to our next meeting. I prepared a non-question, anyway, to let him know that I'd not try it again.

Dick, please do update me on any circumstances pertinent to our situation.

And at that, he shook his head.

There aren't any, I thought it meant.

Or he was lying.

I tried to convince myself that if he was lying, at least it wasn't primarily to me. I would be the thing Dick lied *about*, to Anna, if there was an Anna. He hadn't specifically told me anything about his personal life, so that would mean he couldn't possibly have lied. You have to make a statement in order for it to be false. Of course, he shook his head on the issue of whether he had any circumstances to update me on, that were pertinent to our situation, but that could very well be true. He could not think his home circumstances were pertinent to our situation. It's possible that even if there is an Anna, somewhere behind him in the house, that he isn't doing anything wrong, or that he thinks he isn't doing anything wrong.

Of course, I knew better.

The clock rolled over to eight thirty. There was a message in the inbox about a technical issue, to which I would respond at some point today. Until such a time, I would be considering my response. And of course, I had my meeting. These two tasks would constitute my work for the day.

How absurd it was to even think of them, though, when there were such other existential matters at stake. I assured myself that, even if at any point someone at the organization pointed out that my workload didn't justify the hours, I could point to the existential matters as personal circumstances requiring accommodation. The organization prides itself on accounting for its employees' well-being, not just as employees, but as people.

But these circumstances arose before my employment;

would they be considered pre-existing personal circumstances, ineligible for accommodation?

No, that's a habitual manner of thinking I'd acquired outside the organization. Of course, ongoing issues would be covered.

I wondered whether my issue trusting Dick stemmed from my previous relationship with Maurice. The parallels were certainly obvious enough. Dick was a researcher. Dick made the first move.

Dick maintained online relationships with (other?) women.

And so had Maurice.

Thinking about it, I always cursed myself for not noticing how obvious it was, because of how obvious it wasn't.

Maurice used an email address from a provider known for its adherence to strict security protocols. *Because I value privacy*, he said. In a very abstract sense, I thought he meant. But he meant it very concretely. He meant he valued keeping things secret *from me*. He had pseudonyms on the regular social media sites. He had no browser history.

There was absolutely nothing to be suspicious about, because he had hidden everything suspect.

But I had to check anyway.

It took weeks of shoulder surfing, piecing together his computer login from bits of observations I took care to make at different times, on different days, always making sure to make my movements obvious, looking, looking away, so that he would always be certain I hadn't seen him type the whole thing at any one time.

When I was first hired and completed the organization's security training, I was subjected to additional screening, because of how much I seemed to know about internet security already, and without any formal training. But it was just because I'd been with Maurice.

And then without him.

It turned out Maurice highly valued not only privacy, but also an ugly woman in Florida, whose profile suggested that she honestly enjoyed a man pissing in her mouth. It said a lot of other things too, but now that it's been so long, that's the only detail I recall. I rationalized that those are the sorts of things you have to pretend to enjoy, when you look like that. The thought most present to mind, though, when I thought of her, was every time I'd cleaned Maurice's piss from the floor beside the toilet. Every single time I cleaned the floor, and there was piss there—and it seemed now like it had been *every time*. Had he done it on purpose, imagining he'd put it on a woman? Did he think about me cleaning it and get off on that?

Did he think about *her* cleaning it?

And why didn't he love me?

Maurice thought he hadn't done anything wrong. He explained to me that when you contact someone online, it's not like contacting a real person at all. They're basically inhuman. And you can't be unfaithful except with a person, said Maurice. *There has to be another person involved, and there wasn't.* It would be irrational of me to leave him, he argued, given that I had absolutely no reason to. I told him that's not how it worked—that even if I didn't have a reason to leave him, that I still could. That you can't argue someone into loving you. *And besides, that I was right.* That no matter how right he thought he was, that what I felt still mattered, and that I didn't want to be with someone who hid from me, that I deserved better, that *he was still wrong, they are in fact real people*, though maybe the problem was, ultimately, that he couldn't see any woman as deserving enough to share his whole life with.

I have never understood how it's possible for him to have thought he loved me, and I have never forgiven him for insisting, to the end and beyond, that nevertheless he did.

Thinking of it all over, I thought how terrible of him it was, to pretend all that time, to act as if he'd loved me when he didn't, and how awful he'd probably been to that other woman too. And now to pop up again, as the reason I don't trust Dick. Maurice was really something. How am I supposed to know whether it's Dick who's acting suspiciously, or if it's just Maurice again, reaching forward from the past to ruin my faith in everybody with a cock?

Eight fifty-four.

I got up and went to the washroom, so I wouldn't get stuck for a whole meeting without having peed.

Did Dick not think enough of me to ever mention his (possibly ex-) wife, or did he not think enough of her?

12

SONYA AND MCKENZIE WERE ALREADY IN THE MEETING WHEN I saw the clock move from eight fifty-nine to nine exactly and hit the button to join.

Sonya unmuted her microphone first. The fact that she did meant that this was a matter for management, and that upper management was only here to sign off on the managerial concern. Whatever we were to discuss, it was below McKenzie's level.

Generally, when the three of us met, it was to assign me a task. The task would be something McKenzie wanted done, but because she wasn't my direct manager, she would have to tell Sonya to assign it to me. But also, because she was Sonya's manager, McKenzie would have to supervise Sonya assigning the task to me. It was an ideal system, I thought, because it accidentally allowed me the opportunity to ask clarificatory questions of McKenzie directly, even though it was against protocol to ask clarificatory questions of anyone except one's direct supervisor. I didn't consider that today's meeting would be about anything else, until Sonya began speaking in script.

"Clarissa Knowles, the organization has become aware of a situation regarding your hours of work."

Oh no, I thought. *Was someone in upper management questioning my increased productivity? Were we all about to lose our headsets?*

"Over the past two pay periods, you have claimed over-time on average two point five hours per week. This is a two point five hour increase over your average overtime claims, which in the past have not exceeded zero hours per week, excepting overtime weeks."

Overtime weeks were weeks when the overtime was approved, as when I was completing Devin's calls. Overtime recorded during overtime weeks didn't count as overtime, which kept the organization's overtime expenses down. Human Resources explained to me once that when an employee claims overtime to complete normal work, the orga-nization becomes concerned that the employee is experi-encing a personal circumstance possibly requiring accommodation. But it didn't seem as if Sonya were about to offer any accommodation. McKenzie's silence today seemed not at all procedural, but intentional. Sonya continued.

"The organization would never question whether an employee's use of overtime is legitimate."

Oh god, there it was. A statement of policy. The formal policy regarding the use of overtime from the employee hand-book. It meant Sonya could no longer interact with me as a person—that I had done something to exclude it—that our interactions from here on would be purely formal, an exchange of sentences scripted by the organization with no personal variation and no understanding of mutual goodwill. In my heart, I knew I had just been subject to the worst punishment an employee could receive—a statement of policy without offer of accommodation. With this statement, some-thing would fundamentally change between me and Sonya, between me and the organization. Where I was once a person of potential, I am now a thing to be handled. I had seen it happen before to colleagues, but I never thought it would happen to me. I remember when the office people started logging irregular hours, and the organization had to move them from a scheduled workday to an enhanced productivity tracker to calculate their compensation. I remember how they all had to log into the web portal, accept the policy statement, click consent—how disgraceful it all was, how it was all done under the threat of clarification. I remember thinking how I'd made the right choice moving into the units. I remember that thought coming with a sense of superiority. Now, I regretted every past instance in which I'd assumed that if someone received a policy statement without accommodation, they must have done something to earn it.

"Dr. Knowles, would you like to report any personal circumstances to the organization at this time, which might mitigate this policy statement?"

I had nothing. Even in normal conversations, I always practiced what I would say ahead of time in response to any particular inquiry, and now with the units and the software, I barely ever had to respond to anything on the spot. I thought at once of everything bad that had ever happened to me, and how any of it could be used to explain the overtime. But I didn't want to spring any of that on Sonya. She would be disappointed that I hadn't come to her earlier, that I had conceived of her as the sort of supervisor from whom one should withhold things. But now I had to make up some reason for the overtime that had an attendant reason of why I couldn't mention it, and I just didn't have anything. I *couldn't* have anything, not if I wanted Sonya to look like a good supervisor in front of McKenzie. I couldn't point to any existential matters *after the fact*, not when they'd been affecting my working hours for weeks, without Sonya noticing. Sonya was a good supervisor. I couldn't make it appear as if she wasn't. I just couldn't *do that to her.*

I wish I'd been sent a meeting agenda, so that I'd have known what was coming, could have something to say, but I didn't. All the same, I was wasting time, when I knew what I had to do. I had to accept my fate. I responded:

"There are no personal circumstances."

It was all I could do. In fact, the overtime was logged by the system during my meetings with Dick, and while it counted as liaising with an external stakeholder, it was the organization's policy that such liaisons would take place during regular hours. It was my fault. I had, in fact, done something wrong.

"The organization notes no personal circumstances," Sonya went on. "After this meeting, the employee will receive notification of a new document in her personnel file, on which she must place an electronic signature. The document will serve as evidence of the meeting and its purpose."

I accidentally nodded, even though I knew by now that in this such an official meeting, my responses would have to be verbal.

"I'm sorry," I said, accidentally adding an apology to the record I hadn't meant to. It might be taken as an apology for misconduct, instead of an apology for the nod. I was not having a very good morning. "I will prioritize signing the document over my other duties," I confirmed.

"Then the meeting adjourns," Sonya said, and she was gone. McKenzie was gone. My dignity was gone. I'd never been chastised by the organization before.

It felt like everyone and everything was falling down around me, like supports that had been there until nine o'clock were now not, and I was suddenly alone. I had betrayed McKenzie, and I had betrayed Sonya, and made them appear as if they weren't in complete control of their employees. I was out of control. There was no arguing with it.

When the document appeared, it read exactly as devastatingly as it had sounded during the meeting. I read the sentence in Sonya's voice, and each time I repeated the statement of policy, the voice in which it was expressed lost some of its goodwill, until finally, its tone became hostile. I imagined the hatred in Sonya's eyes as my image of her mouthed the words, again and again.

"The organization would never question whether an employee's use of overtime is legitimate."

13

A BENEFIT OF WORKING IN THE UNITS IS THAT NO ONE BUT management can see you crying at your desk, and then only if they check the monitors. Video of the units outside of the workspace area isn't saved beyond end of day. Even though I'd fallen out with Sonya now, I still trusted her not to look. She was still a good person. I was the one who wasn't.

I read the technical issue that had come into the inbox. A researcher very politely pointed to an error on our front-facing website and had sent us the message "for your information." I knew that in normal parlance that would mean she didn't expect a response. I would respond anyway.

The issue was that there was no way to enter "Physics" as a researcher's field of research. At some point, when the system was designed, the nerds in technical support decided that there would be no way to research "Physics" without specifying a sub-field. The options went "Physics-Mathematical"; "Physics-Quantum"; "Physics-Particle"; and so on. The only way to find out which disciplines were available to choose is to type in "Physics*," where the * was a wild card indicating you wanted the search to return all the sub-fields. But if you entered "Physics," the system would return an error message, "No such field."

"Of course, there's such a thing as Physics," the

researcher had written. "I eventually found the option Physics-Other and was able to save my profile, but I'm sending this for your information."

Of course, *there is such a thing as Physics*, I thought, though I doubted it, given how easily the world could dissipate and everything around us fall part. Nevertheless, I began composing a ticket to technical support. I would suggest to Support that we could, at the very least, make the system warning a little more friendly; instead of "No such field," it could say, "Enter a * after your field to return a list of sub-fields." Tech Support liked it when you suggested specific wording; they could copy and paste the text and minimize the possibility of typos. If you let them come up with the word-ing, or even type something into a document, it was never right. *Never ever ever ever ever.*

What I received in response was something I had never ever seen before.

The email signature stated clearly that the response had come from within the organization, but I didn't recognize the name. They must be a new hire, I thought at first, but the message still concerned me. "Anna Johnstone" from technical support had sent me this message, and I knew it had really come from within the organization, because external messages were clearly marked as such and filtered through the general inbox.

Anna, is that you?

Anna Johnstone from Tech Support had written: "Your issue pertains to the program. Please contact a level 07 officer for a resolution."

But I'm a level 07 officer.

Or was I? Did Anna from Tech Support know something I didn't? Was the punishment for a policy statement now immediate dismissal, but no one had informed me? On the other hand, why would they inform me, if I was no longer an employee? Non-employees don't get notifications. But if I weren't an employee, I shouldn't have been assigned this task. I checked to see if Sonya was online. She was; I could see the green dot indicating her presence. If I weren't an employee anymore, certainly they would have restricted my access to the employee status screen.

Is this some kind of cruel joke, Anna?

It can't be her. It was probably just some new employee who didn't know that they should read the email signatures to figure out who they were talking to before responding. Worse, it was some new employee who didn't want to learn how to do her job, so every inquiry was bounced back to its sender, to figure out a solution. Over time, we would come to know which employees performed their tasks and which weren't worth asking. Perhaps this Anna was one of the latter. It was all a mistake; I wasn't being erased.

Nevertheless, the consideration sent my thoughts spiraling. If I didn't work for the organization anymore, where would I live? I looked around the unit, trying to figure out how many trips it would take to remove my things on light rail transit. Not that there was anywhere I could take them.

I could consult with Syeda.

If I could consult with Syeda, that would prove I still worked here.

"Syeda, are you there?" I typed into the chat.

She immediately appeared on screen. Oh, thank fuck. I explained the issue.

"That's just Tech Support trying to make you do their job for them," Syeda said.

"But I can't do that job for them," I responded. "I don't have access to the backend of the profiles. I don't know how."

"You're not supposed to do their job for them. That's not what I said," Syeda rolled her eyes at me. "Tell Sonya. She will make them do it."

But I didn't want to talk to Sonya. She was probably still angry with me about the overtime.

"Where were you this morning?" Syeda interrupted, as I was trying to figure out how long it would take me to learn the backend of the profiles, so that I could be my own Tech Support.

She meant my meeting. Oh, fuck.

I couldn't tell her about my meeting with Sonya and McKenzie.

"Was it about the 08?" Syeda kept asking. "Is that what the headset is about? I know I'm not supposed to know about that, but if it's got something to do with the 08, I think you'd better say something."

"It's not," I responded, offering no other explanation.

"Are you going for the 08?"

That's what Syeda thought. She thought I was being given special treatment; someone was grooming me as a 08. They gave me the headset so I could present as a person above my current level. It was probably Sonya. She suspected we were in on something together. It wasn't fair.

Syeda had no idea that there was a policy in my personnel file, that I was basically barred from applying for the open 08. I couldn't tell her, either. The organization doesn't discuss personnel files except with the employee whose file it is.

I hung up.

I didn't know what else to do. I'd go offline for half an hour and then say there were technical issues. Syeda would know I was lying. She would assume I was lying about everything—that the 08 was already determined, that it was going to me, that it's why I got the headset in the first place. She would assume that *everything* she had thought to herself was true—that I had betrayed her in applying for her position, that I was Sonya's favourite and would probably get it, that I was Sonya's favourite and would probably get it. When someone else got the position, she'd think it was because they caught on to the favouritism. If *she* ended up with the position.

It hurt as much to think that Syeda would think that of me, as much as it hurt to know that I wasn't Sonya's favourite anymore, not at all—assuming I ever was. Maybe she treated everyone like that. Maybe it was part of the organization's protocol for how managers treat employees. But then, why would Syeda be suspicious of me?

Because I had a headset, and she didn't. Because I couldn't tell her what my meetings were about. I would be suspicious of me too.

I decided not to contact Sonya about the technical issue. I would respond to Anna Johnstone and Anna Johnstone's supervisor, clarifying that I am the level 07 who declared we should have an option for "Physics" as a research field in the profiles. Or at least a friendlier error message telling everyone about the *.

I was shocked to receive an email back almost immediately. And not only was the response negative, Anna's supervisor, Letitia, *had copied Sonya on the reply*.

"The technical support department cannot prioritize this issue, as there has never been a complaint about it."

Never been a complaint about it? I had sent the complaint attached, as evidence that the issue needed a ticket. If it got a ticket, it could be fixed, and that required evidence, so I had sent it. *Never been a complaint?*

Sonya started typing in our private chat.

"Why did you send tech support an issue about which there's never been a complaint?"

"There has been a complaint. I attached it to the bottom of the message. I don't think Letitia scrolled to the bottom."

"Of course, she did. But there's never been a complaint about the issue *before*."

Of course, the distinction that meant the difference about whether we were going to actually deal with an issue.

"There's a complaint now; I sent it."

"Tech support isn't going to devote resources to fix something about which there's never been a complaint *before*."

"What do I do with the researcher's email? Do I tell her there's never been a complaint before?"

"Tell her the organization is exploring options."

"And what do I do with the complaint? Do I file it?"

"I wouldn't do that if I were you. There's no need to make an issue out of something that no one is complaining about."

"Even if no one is complaining about it, it's still an issue. The profiles need to be updated."

"Tech support has bigger problems to solve than some issue from a 07."

The harder she tried to squelch the issue, the more important it seemed to me. How had the organization been getting by all this time, without anyone ever supporting any research in just Physics? Why were we so devoted to sending money to people who were dedicating to themselves to the niche field of Physics-Other? Were there actually many complaints, but each one couldn't be filed away, because of some infinite recurrence of there never having been a complaint *before*? Where was the first complaint on which all the other complaints could rest? Was it non-issues all the way down? And *who the fuck is Anna?*

Why wasn't Sonya taking me seriously?

Because of the policy statement.

I quickly came to realize that I might never have an issue again.

I cried the rest of the afternoon. I typed my response to the researcher through tears, and I didn't pick up when Syeda tried to call back. I sent Sonya a message saying I was taking a personal day, and I signed out of the system. Before I clicked the sign out button, the last thing I saw was a message from Devin Brault, which I figured I could deal with in the morning. The subject was, "Collaboration" (High Priority).

14

I WOKE UP, FED DORIAN, AND LOOKED IN THE MIRROR, thinking, "Is this even my face?"

The foundational premises on which I had lived my life to this point were nothing but social constructions, perishable if left out too long. I wanted to talk to Syeda, but I wasn't sure she would be sympathetic. Certainly, I couldn't tell her what had happened with Sonya and the policy statement. She would only think worse of me for it. Plus, she thought I was after her 08.

The organization that was supposed to be there for me, suddenly it wasn't. If the organization decided against me, I wouldn't get to live in the units anymore. Where could I possibly go now?

Perhaps I could go live in the office. The people in the office were still getting on, still employed, still somehow living. Although we did not know how, there was evidence of their continued existence all over the document revisions. (It is a polite, unspoken policy amongst the unit workers that when an office person makes a document revision, we simply "Reject change" and carry on.) Although I considered this option in the abstract, I knew it could not work. There had never before been an instance of someone moving from the units to the office, not for many months. Either it had never been attempted, or any person who made the attempt was marked for deletion by Tech Support, their name on the version control replaced with another of the same rank. We all suspected but did not discuss aloud the possibility that that was how the office people found their nourishment without having recourse to the restaurants in the tunnels. *Fine*, I thought, *if it comes to that, at least I could provide nutrients to those who are still employed*. But it was not my best option.

After I left Maurice, I'd moved back in with my parents for a while. I'd reduced my material things to a low enough level that they could be integrated into their house, with its decades of accumulation. My basement apartment, from when I first started working at the agency, was pretty bare. When I moved into the units, I reduced my things again. Now looking around the room, I saw very few items around that could constitute my identity, in lack of any external reinforcement. If I reduced just a little more, I could fit them all on one trip on the light rail.

My mother and father had continued to live their lives after I moved in with Maurice. I could tell, when I returned, that there was very little space left for anyone else. They were done with me. It was obvious through every moment. It was one of my main motivations to join the organization; it was supposed to provide an entire way of life, that respected everyone's own way of life. It would allow your individuality and absorb you all at once. It would support your every independent move and by doing so, make you its own.

My father got sick six months after I left for the organization. Before the units existed, I was living in an apartment down the road from the old office. I walked twenty minutes back and forth to work and spoke to my parents sometimes in the evenings. "We're so proud of you," they'd say. *We're so happy you're out*, is what they'd think. They didn't tell me right away, when he got ill. They didn't want to ruin my chances at the organization, my mother said, shortly after he died.

Whatever she went through as he was dying, we'll never know. Three months after he died in hospital, after all his affairs were sorted, the house was sold, and the paperwork all closed, she swallowed a bottle of pills and fell asleep on his grave. There wasn't anything for anyone else to do, when she died. She'd taken care of it all. She'd closed all my father's affairs and her own at the same time. The money went to the humane society. Everything I had been before the organization had disappeared.

Without them, I wasn't anyone. I wasn't anything, and I didn't live anywhere. I was no one, and I had no one. It seemed a bit much that I should have to continue existing in this physical form, when it didn't have a physical place in which to be, and nothing left to do. Even so, I would not feed myself to the office people. At least I had Dorian.

Of course, I hadn't been dismissed.

But my inbox was empty, and no one sent me any more tasks. I waited, for as long as it took, to convince myself that it wasn't just a natural fluctuation in the workload. It wasn't just that McKenzie and Sonya were both busy with something above my level, that they would get back to me soon enough. It wasn't that Syeda just didn't have anything to consult with me about.

The only thing left in my messages was Devin Brault's message, his "Collaboration," which I was saving for when I was sure there was nothing else left.

And then I opened it.

Greetings, Clarissa,
In the interest of collaboration, one of the organization's most closely held principles, I propose a joint effort between us, which would support my career advancement, and quite possibly yours as well.
I submit the attached documents for your review and improvement. Please get them back to me within the week.
Devin.

I looked at the attachments and registered shock in my heartrate. I'll be damned if it wasn't his god damned application to the 08.

Attached to the email were his résumé and cover letter, along with a copy of the posting. Except when I opened the documents, there was very little there. The cover letter was just his name and address, his signature at the bottom, and a short note in the middle, where it said, "Highlight my skills."

What fucking skills, Devin Brault?

I forgot about my predicament and sent a message to Sonya: "Sonya, I've got a message here from Devin, and I'm not sure if it's an appropriate use of my time."

Without asking what it was, she said, "Just do it."

"Really?" I asked, since it seemed the only question left. *Is this real?*

"Have you got anything else to do?"

"Well, no."

"I've got nothing else for you, either. If Devin has something he needs your help with, just do it." As I was formulating a response, she went offline, or possibly invisible. In any case, she was done hearing from me. But she must have sent something to Devin, because a message came through from him almost immediately following.

"Make sure I meet all the qualifications in the posting," he wrote.

I didn't see any point in not saying exactly what I meant at this point.

"You know Syeda is applying for this, right?"

"Yeah, so?"

"You know that she was a United Nations representative to the World Health Organization? That she supervised a team of ten research scientists who created the sustainable energy technology we actually use at the organization?"

"So what?" he wrote in the chat box. "I supervised eleven people in the kitchen."

How could I even respond to that? One, I didn't even think it was true. Maybe if you took into account multiple shifts and counted everyone who worked in the kitchen throughout the days, evenings and weekends. There's no way there was ever eleven people in the kitchen at once. Besides that, it doesn't fucking count against what Syeda has done. Why was Devin Brault unable to tell that he was obviously deficient, compared to the needs of the position? Why would the organization even consider his application? Shouldn't there be a stop-check, at some point in the application, to make sure some 02 wasn't trying to elevate to a 08 without any of the relevant experience? Of course, there had to be. Someone would check. Thinking about it, I figured that someone must be checking over these documents, before the application would get serious consideration by anyone. There's got to be a qualifying round, to make sure the applications met the minimum requirements, before pool of *real* applicants would be determined. There had to be. Assuring myself of this, I didn't answer him specifically. Instead, I said, "I'll get in touch if I have any questions," and I resolved to take the matter into my own hands.

Devin would have his documents by the end of the week.

15

DORIAN AND I SPENT TWO DAYS ON DEVIN BRAULT'S COVER letter. The résumé spoke for itself. He had a GED, and he started working as a cook shortly after dropping out of high school, rising to the rank of kitchen manager after only twelve short years.

I went through each of the qualifications listed on the job posting, and I wrote in the cover letter how Devin Brault met that qualification. Where the job posting read, "At least three years' of research production gaining international repute," I wrote, "I was indirectly responsible for a lot of people eating food for several years, some of which were probably tourists from different countries." Where the job posting said, "Supervision of a team of ten or more specialists in my discipline," I wrote, "I was a kitchen manager in a kitchen with eleven staff members, some of whom I supervised some of the time." The end result was pretty repetitive, as Devin's experience was sparse. Where the job posting demanded that someone, "Have at least ten years' experience in targeted communications appealing to a variety of stakeholders," I wrote, "As kitchen manager, I talked to both staff and customers on a regular basis, as well as my own friends and family after hours."

I kept assuring myself that everyone else would read the

same résumé that I was reading, that while I made sure every box was ticked, anyone able to read would know that *not really*. I had to rephrase every qualification to make it about Devin's time at the restaurant. He didn't have any research experience. He didn't work in communications. He didn't supervise any specialists.

I sent Dick Richards a link to my personal room on video chat. I briefly considered how much it would matter if I kept allowing the system to track overtime, given my status as pariah. Maybe I should make out with as much money as possible. I tried to calculate how much money I could make on overtime before being necessarily dismissed, as compared to how much money I would make if I stayed on for as long as possible, being careful not to break any other rules, but the variables were too many and too complex to work out. At the same time, I figured that as long as I was working on Devin's application, I was still working for the organization.

In its best interests.

Dick and I didn't talk out loud, but I imagined everything he might say about my situation, if we did.

He would laud my ingenuity, taking over Devin's application to the 08, but making sure to do it in such a way that it couldn't possibly get anywhere.

He would admire my writing, down to the sentence level, recognizing that my word choices always bordered on synonyms of qualifications, but never enough to ascertain any equivalency to the posting's requirements.

Above all, he would value how loyal I stayed to Syeda, despite how she questioned my integrity and my intentions. Because *he too valued loyalty*, I imagined.

You're a good friend, a good writer, and a good person, Dick would say.

All he ever actually said out loud was, "Uhhhhhhh-hhhhhhh."

PART THREE

16

My meetings with Dick became routine. He would log on at the same time and log off fifteen minutes later, spent. I quit trying to make it interesting for him. He didn't care. I didn't care. Maybe there was an Anna, and maybe there wasn't. Everything with Dick moved routinely. I started counting his strokes on camera, and I developed a spreadsheet tracking their development over time. So far, the relationship was linear, slope of zero—on average, of course. Dick was neither growing impatient with me nor unable to climax due to boredom. Mathematically, we were fine.

For three weeks, I'd been keeping all my belongings in a rolling duffel bag by the door. Despite the union's regulations, in the lack of any specific tasks, I always felt my dismissal was imminent. I hoarded cash. Whenever I went to get a Diet Coke, I'd stick my card in the machine, pretend it didn't work, and then use the bank machine right next to it to get out twenty dollars. I'd buy my soda, pocket the change, and go back to my room. I had almost three hundred dollars in twonies in an old Crown Royal bag at the bottom of my duffel. I imagined that when I left, I'd tie it to my belt— except that I wouldn't, for fear of the looks I'd get on the light rail.

I didn't think I'd actually have to make the decision to leave.

Who would leave the organization?

It's so hard to get in, and then the situation is so good. Sure, there are people who move between departments, get bored every few months, start a new contract, try to work their way up the levels. And there are people who retire. Come to think of it, I don't know anyone who's *just left*. I'm not sure there's even a process for it.

I had no choice, though.

We had a meeting, and I was invited. Somehow, I had recently been left out of the calendar invites to our weekly meetings. I sent a message to Sonya about it, but I couldn't tell if it was read. That gave me plausible grounds to let the issue slide. If they weren't going to invite me to the meetings, and I had told them of their mistake, then they couldn't blame me for not attending. I had the records to prove it. The links changed every week, for security purposes, and I didn't have them. I surely couldn't be blamed.

So when I got the invitation to a "Special Business" meeting, forwarded by Devin Brault, of course I had to go. Otherwise, I would no longer be blameless.

I put on my best clothes. In my spare time, I'd been ordering newer pieces, which would come to the units via courier. For our meeting, I knew they couldn't see farther down than my shoulders (unless I sat farther back from the camera, which would in itself seem strange). I chose a black leather blazer with feathered white shoulders.

The image would suggest to them that I was innocent.

Even if they were cynical, the image would suggest that I, at least, *thought* that I was innocent, and then they would have to question what my reasons were for believing so, eventually coming to the conclusion that I might have a good reason for that belief. I *do* have good reason for that belief.

I'd gotten over the guilt of using overtime hours to talk to Dick Richards. It was McKenzie who told me to in the first place. Our researchers need resources. We have the resources available. If the organization wanted to argue that we didn't have the resources for the overtime, what might their argument be? That they didn't have the money? They couldn't make that argument. It would throw the entire research community into turmoil.

They had the money, and they told me to use it, and I did. That's that.

Syeda was another story.

If she wouldn't assume the worst about everyone, she could have reasoned out that I wasn't about to take her new position. I didn't want it. I hadn't worked for it. There was no way I would get it. Did she think I was that stupid, to try for something I couldn't possibly get, or that mean, to take it away from her? She should think better of me.

They should all think better of me.

Under the jacket, I wore a blouse that went up to my neck, vertical rainbow stripes, with white and black as well. I straightened my hair, like I was taking a picture for my employee profile and wanted it to look professional. In full makeup, black eyeliner to show them I'm serious, red lipstick to show them I'm confident, I went online five minutes before the meeting time, a move that could be conceived of as aggressive, given that it was our policy not to join meetings early—it was a waste of the organization's time. But so was I, and I was feeling a little aggressive about it. So be it.

Five minutes later, the meeting began. Sonya spoke first.

"The host has turned off the cameras of everyone observing, so that we might all focus on the candidates." So they'd never see my visual preparations. Well, fuck.

Syeda and Devin Brault appeared, each dressed in simple black, as was required whenever we were evaluating candidates for an open position, so that we might focus on their qualifications and not their outfits.

"Of the candidates to the 08 officer position, two have submitted explanations for how they meet every qualification that the job posting demands. We have Devin Brault and Syeda Bey. This meeting will determine whose qualifications best fit the position, in an open and transparent manner."

Oh god, what have I done? My collaboration with Devin

was over so long ago, I had assumed Syeda would be in her new position by now, and that her new disdain for 07's was contributing to her overall neglect of our relationship.

But apparently, she hated me in particular.

She couldn't know I had written Devin's cover letter, though. He couldn't have told her. They didn't talk. If the job had ever come up, and Syeda found out he was applying, that was all the more reason not to talk. There's no way she could know. I questioned myself and my own moral worth for worrying about whether Syeda had found out, rather than worrying what kind of a person I was for doing it in the first place. But I had been in a situation. There was nothing I could do.

No, Maurice would have said. *There's always something you can do.*

Like what? I screamed at him to answer, as the meeting continued, unheard by me.

You know you don't have to be there, right? Maurice would have said.

You mean leave? I knew the answer. I already knew.

You could try that, his voice, as I remembered it, a little deeper than before. *Before you kill yourself.*

But that wasn't Maurice talking, was it? It was me. I always knew there was a way out, and I wouldn't leave. I would rather fuck over a friend than leave the organization, and I knew that was true, because *it was what I had done.*

Now Syeda was talking: "… I am clearly the only candidate to this position, and it's absurd to compare the records of two such people as myself and Devin Brault. There's no question about who should be promoted to level 08." As she finished, I lamented how we'd never had the opportunity to discuss how she would go about this meeting. We could have strategized. Now here she was, not answering the questions the organization presented during its evaluations, assuming her competence would be evident, though the organization only cares about what you can demonstrate with the available documentation. She was likely taken off guard at being pitted against Devin in the first place, and was currently working through her resentment, even as she tanked her chances. She should have gone through her record of service, presented evidence to the decision makers. She should know that *anything that wasn't presented at the meeting didn't count*, and that it was completely possible to be eliminated as a candidate if the executives found the presentation lacking. She was thrown off. It wasn't right.

Even so, I didn't think Devin would be able to talk his way through his part of the candidacy process, given how few qualifications he had and how short a time he'd been with the organization. Even if Syeda failed this evaluation, and she certainly had, Devin should fail more memorably.

Sonya asked Devin to summarize the argument for his promotion.

"I should get this job for two reasons," Devin said into the camera. His black shirt had white buttons. I didn't recall the policy for what colour his buttons should be; perhaps there wasn't one.

"One reason is that I'm also obviously qualified, or else I wouldn't be in this interview. I wouldn't have applied for the position if I weren't qualified," he said with a smirk. "The other reason I should get the job over Syeda is that I have experience supervising eleven people, which is more than her."

Not even the sentence was correct. Of course eleven people are more than Syeda; she's only one person. He should have said *more than she has*. The executives should notice the mistake. Oh god, maybe this was her way out!

Instead, they asked Syeda, "How large was your research team at the United Nations?"

Syeda looked sick. She didn't answer for a moment. If it were me, I would be considering whether I should lie. But then I would consider that the organization always verified statements made in evaluations, and I would advise myself against it. Finally, she would decide that even with the smaller team, her qualifications should obviously exceed any of Devin Brault's, and that it was all right to tell the truth.

"I supervised a research team of ten people," she said. "We worked on the——"

"Please no supplementary statements," McKenzie interrupted her. "Supplementary statements disqualify a candidate from proceeding with the evaluation."

Sonya continued: "The candidates will now be removed from the evaluation, so the executives might discuss their presentations."

With Syeda and Devin gone, they did discuss.

"A level 02 shouldn't be considered for a level 08."

"He explained how he met the qualifications."

"It's not clear that he did, though."

"The explanation is right there."

"What about the other candidate?"

"A level 08 must always conduct themselves with honesty and integrity."

"Her experience speaks for itself."

"None of that is relevant at the meeting stage."

"If he weren't qualified for the position, he wouldn't have applied!"

"His team was larger than hers was; it's the only discernible difference we can use to make this decision."

"Surely you don't believe that."

"What it comes down to is that eleven is greater than ten."

"Is eleven greater than ten, in this case?"

"Unfortunately, so."

"Bring them back."

Syeda and Devin reappeared on screen. Syeda looked visibly ill. Devin appeared unconcerned. He had no stake in this game.

McKenzie spoke: "The executives have determined that eleven is more than ten."

Syeda looked horrified. She was about to make a statement when she thought better of it and shut her mouth. She knew all was lost and was already considering the next opportunity. Candidates who misbehaved in evaluations weren't afforded other opportunities.

"Devin Brault will be elevated to level 08."

Was this always a possibility? It had to have been. Then why did it seem as though things kept happening that were impossible?

"Would you like to make an acceptance statement?"

There was no chance he wouldn't accept. No chance at all.

"I would," Devin started, sitting a little higher on his screen.

"I would like to thank the board for recognizing my experience to be just as valid as anyone else's within the organization. You have today demonstrated an open-mindedness that I had believed was long lost, especially here, and among people like you. I'm glad to see that your judgments have not been clouded by tradition. After so long working as an 02"— it had not even been a year at this point—"I feel my promotion comes just on time, if not already too late, though I understand our processes take some time. It's one of the things I'll work on in my new position."

He went on: "I would like to extend my goodwill to Syeda, whose gracious defeat I expect she will recognize as the inevitable conclusion of a fair and just, *merit-based* promotion process—that while I'm sure she might qualify, should another 08 position open in the future, it should be clear to all that in this particular competition, she was simply outmatched, as was obvious to every *objective* evaluator taking part in this process."

Oh Syeda, I wish we had just talked.

I wish anyone had spoken to me, actually. Anyone at all.

Except for Devin Brault. He went on.

"Finally, I'd like to reassign Clarissa Knowles as my personal second officer, as she truly believed in my qualifications throughout my long road to promotion."

My camera turned on, and there I was, wings and colours and all, like I was waiting to make a scene.

Sonya spoke: "Dr. Knowles, do you accept your assignment?"

I panicked.

"Technical issues," I said, and took several seconds, on camera, to disconnect the power, the Wi-Fi, the backup wired internet connection, and to remove battery from my machine. "Technical issues," I said again, to affirm the obvious lie. "Technical issues," I said once more, even though I was sure no one was left to hear me.

"Technical issues," I mumbled to myself as the tears came and went. "Technical issues," I said, slapping myself in the face, as if the pain would make the tears stop moving. Syeda would never forgive me now. Sonya would think me ridiculous. McKenzie would laugh. *Serves her right*, they would say. "Technical issues," I whispered to Dorian as I plucked his claws from the sides of his carrier, all the better to place him inside. There were technical issues with the whole process, I determined, the phrase repeating itself in my head, long after the tears had stopped, and I looked around for anything left either of my or of Dorian's things.

I *had to* leave.

I had no choice.

17

I submitted a "Conflict of Interest" form, letting the organization know that I had developed a conflicting interest. It was the closest form I could find to a resignation.

I printed the address for Dick's historical house, and I put it in my pocket, just in case I should die on the way, and someone should wonder where I was going, and check. In another jacket pocket, I put the transit directions to Dick's. I had my phone, of course, but I didn't know how well it would connect outside the organization's Wi-Fi zone. Once the light rail left the island, the city Wi-Fi would kick in—or would it? It's been months since I've tried. Before I walked out the door, I took some twonies out of my bag and put them in my pockets, ten on one side, ten on the other. My pants jangled, but if I kept my hands in my pockets and held the coins, not all that much, and besides, I might need them.

Just in case.

Now the people in the hall might be another issue. I hadn't gone anywhere but the soda machine in months. If there existed anyone in the hallway as I was departing, they'd see me with the duffel in one hand and Dorian in the other, and they'd wonder what I was up to. But also, if they saw me looking up and down the hall in both directions before I left, or worse, doing that and then waiting for them to leave, they'd be suspicious.

But you know, there's only one way to handle these situations, and it's to do what you want to do and look like you mean it. I can walk down whatever hallways I want to, and it's none of their fucking business.

Plus, if they ask, I can just say I'm going to visit my parents.

My dead parents?

My ghost parents, fuck off.

Who would actually remember that my parents were dead, anyway? Nobody around here gives a fuck about a personal detail like that.

Are you doing your job, or are you not doing your job? That's all anyone needed to know about you.

I am not, not today. I'm getting on the bus to go to Dick's.

Then I'll figure everything out. I'll figure out whether or not he has a bigger lexicon than *Uhhhhhhnnnnnnnn.* Then I'll know whether there's an Anna or not. Then I'll know whether or not you come inextricably intertwined with anyone with whom you've shared some certain intimate moments, and then I'll know whether Maurice meant it, or he didn't, when he said that nobody else he met online meant anything to him.

Fuck of a way to learn, though.

Most of all, I had to get away from Devin Brault, before he could assign me any tasks. I could not be subordinate to Devin. I absolutely could not submit. Things there have gone far enough already. At any moment now, the deciding thing could come—that thing where once it's done, it can't be undone, and I'm stuck living that life forever, being that person, that tool. Devin Brault's second.

Who gives a fuck who's in the hallway, when these are the stakes?

A light rail, followed by a short walk, followed by a bus, followed by a second short walk. It's been long time since we've gone that far, but I looked at Dorian in his carrier, and he looked at me like he trusted I was making the right move, and that was that.

Dorian was a lot lighter than my duffel, which I wasn't counting on. He has one of those carriers that's also like a duffel, soft, not hard, and I didn't account for the fact that the contents would be the difference. I was hoping the weights would be symmetrical, at least, to make the burdens even, at least. But *that's how it is*, I told myself. *Get used to it.* I've adapted to worse. For a few minutes, it's going to be uncomfortable. But after that, it'll be like that's how it's always been.

Just a new level of normal discomfort.

And I've played that game before.

Dorian changed his mind, though, the second I picked him up. He wasn't upset, necessarily, but certainly concerned about where we were going, and he emitted his queries at a consistent rate from within his carrying case. I knew the thickness of the doors wouldn't squelch the sounds, so that not only anyone in the hallways, but also anyone in their units, would know that a cat had passed by.

What of it, though?

I looked around the room several times to make sure I wasn't leaving anything of myself behind. Besides the customizations to the room itself, which were the property of the organization, I had everything I owned on my person.

Now that's freedom.

Heavy fucking freedom, though.

At least in the hallways, I was in motion. The act of propelling myself forward distracted me from the weight and would discourage anyone from talking to me, as if they wanted to talk to me, they would have to stop me first.

And they couldn't.

I made it all the way to the elevators and pressed the button.

If anyone were leaving at this time of day, they'd be going down to the restaurants. But I had farther to go. I wish I had picked a unit on a lower floor, so there'd be fewer stops on the way down, but alas.

I had wanted to live so high that there weren't insects

anymore. Someone when I was young said that was the seventh floor or above. Who knows if they were right. I didn't open the windows, anyway. Never had.

On the fifth floor, we were stopped.

Funny, in my imagination it was always some interrogative stranger whom I encountered on my way out of the units. Some nosy person whose strangeness to me made them more comfortable asking questions that no real friend would ask. But when the elevator doors opened to let this person on, it wasn't the unfriendly stranger at all. It was Amira.

I hadn't seen her in physical form since the office opened.

She looked more or less the same, a little older. If we were still in the office, perhaps I'd notice more little differences. I used to be able to tell, pretty well, when someone bought new shoes or got a haircut. But now it all happens automatically, and I've no differences to point out to make conversation. So I said, "Hello, Amira."

"Hello!" she said. "Heading out for a vacay?"

Now the thing about people whom I did know, is that I knew they were too polite to inquire further. Really, this was a much better scenario than the interrogative stranger.

"Yeah, I had some time coming to me."

"And you can only roll that over five years, you know," she said.

"I do know; it was part of orientation."

"Yeah, they say it, but when the time comes, it's still hard not to feel like you're being forced out, you know? I spent my last vacation in my room just hiding from the workspace camera."

We laughed.

"Now what kind of vacation lets you bring your cat along?" she asked.

Oh fuck.

Oh nevermind, it's fine.

"Oh, haha," I enunciated. "Actually, Dorian's off to Camp Grandma's."

Amira looked at me, as she performed the calculations. It could be the name of an established business entity; she wouldn't know. It could be my actual parents or grandparents; I couldn't remember how much she knew.

"Oh, I get it," she says. "I forgot you're funny."

We stood in silence the rest of the way down. It was the comfortable silence of the first few minutes of a virtual meeting, when we're allowing a short grace period for everyone to log on. Amira was in another department; she wouldn't know anything about what was going on in mine. That's how we compartmentalized, for the sake of security. We could have been good friends if I had tried at all. But it's too late.

I felt an imaginary loss all the same.

18

Outside, waiting for the light rail, I looked back at the office building. I was alone at the designated stop. I wondered how many people came and went anymore. Even if no one did, it would take months for the light rail system to adjust. I was thankful that it hadn't.

Looking at the office building, I saw that the windows had been papered over. "Natural light" was supposed to have been a selling point of the building. The office people did not seem to think so. I wonder what in their new makeup made the light unbearable. Or perhaps it was a security measure to stop people outside from using telescopes to read their screens. Through the standard issue discount kraft paper we used to use to send boxes of written communications to members and stakeholders, I should have at least been able to see movement, some flickering of light as the office people moved about or even changed the views on their monitors, but there wasn't any. The desolation of the invisible insides of that building felt creepy, like in its perception I was gaining access to a dark element of human nature that best remained hidden. Then finally the rail car arrived.

I would be on the light rail for eight stops, including the final stop. At the front of the rail car, there was a blue-haired girl with a broom, and I smiled at her. I remembered some past moment when I'd just moved into a place during school. I'd met some people in classes and not gotten to know anyone, and also I didn't have everything I would need, so when I dropped a glass bottle covered in condensation on the kitchen floor and didn't have a broom, I sat down in it and cried, thinking of how life's not worth living without a broom. Then this girl sees me through the open door and loans me one. I couldn't remember what she looked like. It was easy to imagine they were the same person, that this blue-haired girl was on her way to save someone like me.

A straight couple was fighting, because he'd spent some money they didn't have. A man with a golden retriever pulled it closer, obviously uncomfortable with the aggressive tones. The girl with the broom faded into the background as my consciousness became absorbed in this man's discomfort, the couple's voices getting louder and louder as the rest of the train realized that whatever its concerns, those concerns wouldn't be voiced today, not on this ride. Even Dorian stopped asking where we were going.

"You're causing a scene," he argued.

"Don't change the subject. We're not arguing about who's causing scenes and who isn't."

"We could discuss this later."

"I won't be as angry, then."

"That's kind of the point."

"You think I should shut up until I'm not angry anymore?"

"No, that's not what I'm saying."

All the while, she seemed impervious to the outside gazes of the people around, while his perceptions shifted from them to her and back again. Her focus of attention was more powerful. I anticipated she would win the argument and always would.

Second stop.

The girl with the broom got off, and I wanted to follow her, as she was my only friend. I couldn't get close to the man with the dog; you know how these tentative people are. One day you're protecting them, and the next day you hurt them too.

Now I know you're not supposed to weigh in on problems in other people's departments, but I couldn't help but form an opinion about the couple's argument. And I think others on the train were doing the same. (I was trained that it's fine to have these opinions, but not to present them on behalf of the organization; at the organization, we represent the organization's policies, not our own opinions). At the same time, it seemed like the man's expense was in fact an eligible expense, but the woman had underestimated the required budget allocation.

This all could have been solved if the budget justification were submitted in advance and reviewed by the committee members. There are people whose job it is to determine what is and isn't an appropriate expense—what sorts of things to spend money on, and how much money is appropriate to any of those particular things. And for cases outside the realm of normal, an argument can always be advanced for why the expense is justifiable, given the context and objectives of the project.

But these people had no system in place at all. No policies, no review process. From what I gathered from this brief interaction, expenses were deemed eligible based on who was more willing to cause or not cause a scene on the train. I'm sure once the matter is settled, no one will even record it as precedent, for the judgment of future expenses.

How do people function out here? It's fucking chaos already.

Four stops.

What would become of us all, if all policy were determined by the loudest voice on the rail car?

The man with the dog was getting more nervous, like he expected the couple to turn on him at any moment, ask him for his opinion, settle it for them. He couldn't be expected to be judge and jury. No matter what decision he made, someone would be angry with him. He preferred nobody be angry with him. It was clear he wasn't thriving in this environment, and I wondered what was so important to him, that he remained where he was, that he got here in the first place.

What was his trajectory?

Why was he on this train?

Some people just aren't suited for public transit.

It's the same group of people who are forced onto public transit—the meek, the anxious, the indigent, the people who didn't succeed according to capitalism's standards and are probably living on government stipends, who are expected to take *mass transit*, because it's cheaper, because *all they are is mass*, but it's really an ironic stab in the throat, because the whole idea was first to recognize that there shouldn't exist certain people out, in and amongst the masses, and then by recognizing that, to force them there.

Thus the dog. Dogs are for people who like or dislike humans or both. The dog is a second body for the anxious man to take refuge in. A second set of eyes but also a thing with which to exist in relation.

He had every right to have it.

But the woman wasn't satisfied with only winning one argument.

She started, in a voice meant to project to a larger audience than one: "Ugh, my allergies—"

Six stops.

Then she paused, because no one would be able to pay attention to her whining during the transfer on and transfer off of the new and former transit riders. The man with the dog knew what was coming, but unfortunately, it wasn't his time to depart. He very likely had somewhere to be, somewhere that couldn't wait for him to leave the train, wait for the next one, get back on, continue without being passively-aggressively victimized by someone themselves claiming victim status. The organization recognized the phenomenon, and it was strictly forbidden. Ever since the installation of gender-neutral washrooms, when Chantal organized a protest, claiming that the installation would somehow victimize her. Even in those early days, the organization recognized that you can't claim oppression in order to oppress people, and Chantal's protest received the closest thing there is to a dismissal—a mandatory training module to prevent behaviour like hers. But this woman, as we've already covered, had apparently missed the mandatory training module on that.

She started again. "Ugh, my allergies—does someone on this train have an animal? I can't be around *dogs*," she declared, a tone of mock suffering in her voice. "You know I can't!" She turned and looked at the dog-man, but the "you" was addressed to her partner. The timid man put an arm around his dog and pulled it closer, as if the inch would help.

I hoped that she did have allergies, and I hope that it was Dorian making her suffer. But she didn't see the little grey kitty in front of my seat; she saw the big yellow dog and the timid man nearby, and she was out for blood. I wonder what timid men have ever done to her to deserve such mistreatment, but I reminded myself, that's not the way it works. No matter who had hurt her, the timid men were going to pay. But as for the original cause, it could have been anyone.

"Maybe you could talk to him and see if he can't do something about his *DOG*," she said to her boyfriend/spouse/manfriend/first victim, but loud enough, again, for everyone to hear. Loud enough to try and make that poor man ashamed just for living. Loud enough that something in me stirred, and I concluded that someone would have to stand up for the human good. Someone would have to instill in her the civility and respect that characterized a progressive work environment.

Even if that someone was me.

This is exactly why I didn't want to go into management.

You've got to push me a little bit before I get the urge to handle people.

But here we are.

I tried to think of a policy statement that would put her in her place.

Before I could, though, I had to deal with a new form of devastation.

Slowly making its way across the floor of the train,

reacting to turns, the accelerations and the decelerations, and the interfering movements of the passengers trying to stand on the exact same bits of floor, was a trail of putrid liquid.

And its origin was undeniably Dorian's travel bag.

I could see the fact of it register on the nearby faces as they formulated their responses. The man with the dog, relieved the attention would be drawn from him. The dog, interested in what this other animal had done and perhaps considering his own bladder's needs. The man with the woman, dreading what his partner might have to say about this new situation. The woman herself, eyes wide, happy, finally satisfied there was something to be actually angry about and someone who deserved her wrath.

None of the potentialities foretold in their looks would come to fruition.

Like the light from a heaven in which people used to believe, the door opened, and fluorescence poured through.

It was my stop.

The tribulations of this world were left behind as I jumped through the doors and walked a safe distance away from them, on the platform, heading towards the stairs that would lead me back down to ground level, a new life, a new social circle, or preferably, none at all.

I stopped and crouched down, so that Dorian could see me.

"I'm sorry," I told him. "It has become evident that I did not account for your needs. But I hope we'll both find somewhere comfortable to be soon enough." At least Dorian wouldn't spend the rest of his journey uncomfortable, having to relieve himself and having nowhere to do it. He's solved that problem for the both of us. There was still some urine in his bag, and some had soaked his fur, but most of it was left behind on that train, would be cleaned at the end of the night with one of those big hoses, gone.

It was a short walk to the bus stop.

19

OFF THE TRAIN, I WAS GRATEFUL THAT THE WORLD IS BIG enough that there are some people you meet once and never see again. I was happy to be rid of the train people. Even if I did sympathize with the man who had the dog, I knew we would never be any kind of friends. Even so, though it was easy enough never to see strangers again, it still seemed unfair that I should be forced into association with all sorts of other people, just as much by chance, not of my own volition. People who would keep coming back, people who would change the course of my life, when I didn't even mean to meet them—their existence seemed unfair. I wished there was a train to get off of with respect to those people, and then I laughed, because there is, and it's death.

I arranged myself for the walk from the train to the bus. It was five blocks straight up the street, as long as I initially chose the correct direction. It was hard, knowing which way to go from unfamiliar landmarks, so I had memorized the route based on explicit instructions I gave myself by looking at the satellite pictures of the route online. The problem was, I had escaped from the light rail platform in such a hectic fashion, that I no longer knew which exit I had used, and which side of the street I was on. With my belongings on one shoulder and Dorian on the other, whom I now had to hold at an angle to keep the wetness away from my person proper, I couldn't afford to fuck around.

At least I still looked respectable, in the clothes I had chosen for what turned out to be Devin Brault's interview. But I had worn my nice shoes. I had a second pair in my bag, for the future, when I didn't have to impress anyone as much. I considered wearing those shoes for the duration of the journey, but I knew from experience that I would find no convenient place to switch them out before I got to Dick's house, so I'd better leave in the shoes I planned to arrive in. The nice ones that hurt.

I picked a direction and went with it. If it was wrong, I'd figure it out at the next corner. But you know what, it wasn't, so by the end of the first block, I could already quit using my lack of awareness of my location as an excuse not to think about what would happen when I arrived at the house of Dick Richards.

In my run-throughs, the situation as I had imagined it so many times in preparation, Dick would ask me what I was doing there. But after so many times trying to explain, and not being able to do so in a way he would understand and which I could express within a timeframe appropriate to how long someone should be standing immediately outside another person's door, he stopped asking. He would just be happy to see me.

I would approach the house from the eastern side. It would be dark by then. In the satellite imagery, I saw a shrub on the eastern side of the house, facing a neighbour's windowless siding. Before I made my move, no one would acknowledge an out-of-place woman walking, as I would walk with purpose. But as I approached the side of the house with this shrub, I would change my demeanor, just for a moment, because efficiency is more important than attitude for this operation. This is the part where I hide my bag and Dorian's behind the shrub, before I knock on the door.

Dorian should be weary from travel by then and, since he normally slept a large part of the day, I was hoping the journey, followed by the first sense of stability he'd felt since probably this morning, would be enough to ensure his exhaustion. He would sleep, as I assured for us both a safe place to stay, and then he would forgive me for leaving him in a bush for hours, before finally forgetting the whole ordeal.

With Dorian and my bag in the bush, I would knock on the door. Dick Richards would answer, a tea towel slung over his shoulder, as he'd just been washing up after dinner. "No thank you, I've eaten," I'd lie as he welcomed me, old friends, intimate partners, just dropping by, as one does.

He'd offer me a glass of wine, and we'd talk about us and where we were going. We would laugh about all the awkward moments so far, and how good it was of me to stop by and finally resolve any sense of the unknown overshadowing the development of our relationship. About three hours in, during the second bottle of wine, I'd ask him about Anna. He would admit how she broke his heart, and how he hadn't been able to find anyone to fully understand, until I had come along. How I had given him exactly what he needed, exactly when he needed it, and how from here to eternity, he'd be grateful for my presence during the most difficult time of his life.

Near the end of the second bottle, I'd make sure we opened a third, and while Dick would protest, I'd tell him it's all right. I really want to continue talking, so I'd be willing to stay the night, if that's what it takes. About halfway through that bottle, I'd admit that I had some extra baggage to bring in. I had it with me thanks to some unrelated travel, and because of some adorable neuroses, had hit it in the bush before knocking on the door. Dick would be too inebriated at this point to consider physical intimacy, and I'd tell him that it's fine, go to bed, I'll figure my own way around. And I'd locate the already made-up guest bedroom, where Dorian and I could finally be alone, away from everyone, but with Dick nearby, in case we needed him. I would notice the stale smell of the linens, and I'd put it on my list of things to take care of while I was there, as one takes care of the environment in which one makes their home.

From there, the rest would have to be figured out, as it's impossible to speculate.

Dorian, meanwhile, did not like the to and fro of my pace as I walked past the fourth block intersection, keeping between the pedestrian lines, and he indicated so with his cries. Anyone who looked at me would know I wasn't pedestrian. If anyone did notice me out of place in Dick's neighbourhood, they might consider it an honour I was there, dressed as I was.

Of course, never should I ever have allowed myself to think such hubristic thoughts, because the moment I did, my pant leg, shifted down because of the twonies in my pockets, or perhaps because of the rubbing of bags on either side of my waist, caught itself under the heel of my nice shoe, creating out of nothing something for me to trip over, such that from the perspective of anyone watching from the road or from inside their houses, I simply fell over, for no reason at all. The hem of my pants and I both ruined in a single step.

20

Before I stood up, I checked Dorian. He was not crushed by my body in the fall, as I had imagined. But he was upset. He was upset at seeing me so degraded, but also relieved, as now he was not the only one between us who was physically filthy.

My arms hurt from being crushed under me, as I'd apparently tried to break my fall, only to discover that the weight on both sides of my body was too much, causing too great an acceleration. My arms retracted like a t-rex, trying to hold the bags in place as I fell to the ground, face-first, my wrists taking most of the hit. My twonies were everywhere. Thank goodness for the organization's supplemental health coverage covering acts of self-sabotage.

And then I remembered, I wouldn't have access to it anymore, not if I were leaving forever. But then, I'd only submitted a conflict of interest form. Perhaps my departure wouldn't be official until morning, in which case the accident would have taken place during the coverage period. I might even argue that it was caused by mental distress at work, and that it should therefore be considered a work-related injury.

The considerations subsided as I realized that while my wrists would certainly swell, I might not need their coverage after all.

I could decide *not* to need it.

The feeling of freedom washed over me as I laid psychological claim to my wounds. They weren't anyone else's problem but mine.

Even if I died from them, that was a choice I could choose, if I so chose.

Of course, if I thought they were all that bad, I might have thought differently.

On my walk covering the final block to the bus stop on route to Dick's house, I ascertained that none of my injuries were preventing my motion. I could continue to move as I liked, or more accurately, I was condemned to. If only for some time might my options be taken from me; what a freedom that would be. But with mixed feelings, I confirmed that time wasn't now.

All the same, when I arrived at the sign indicating that this was the stop for the 20 and that I had seventeen minutes to wait, I despaired at how this bus stop wasn't of the quality to which I had become accustomed at the organization, and I sat down on the wet grass out of spite. There was nothing here; no benches, no shelter, no button to activate the rapid heat function, nothing but a post stuck in the ground.

What has our society come to?

I knew, because I'm self-aware, that if it weren't for the fall a block ago, I wouldn't even care. But the lack of amenities at this public transit stop, I genuinely perceived as the fall of humanity. The story of how Dick's and my evening would go was becoming ever more implausible, the worse my physical appearance degraded. At the same time, I couldn't just decide to go back. I'd come too far already, made too many decisions in the same direction—away from the organization and toward Dick Richards' house. The time for reconsiderations had already passed, back when I determined that my injuries wouldn't suffice to serve as an excuse for such a drastic reversal. Now that I had discovered a benchless bus stop—suddenly that was reason enough to balk?

No, I decided, as the bus arrived. If I didn't get on now,

the driver would be upset; after all, he'd stopped the entire vehicle already, just for me.

21

I PAID THE FARE.

The bus driver didn't look askance at my ruined hem, my extra baggage, the smell of Dorian's fabric cage. She assumed I must be one of those people. I wanted so badly for her to look me in the eye, exchange the compulsory greetings, which the organization recognizes as integral to an employee's sense of recognition and identity. She didn't. I knew the mandate of her organization demanded polite and courteous transactions, but I didn't know if she was breaking any rules by not making eye contact.

Rules don't regulate behaviour, anyway. I mean they do, but they don't. Even if there was a rule in favour of eye contact, nobody could force her, at this point, to have made it.

I looked around the rest of the bus for someone else to recognize me.

Please see that I'm not the person I am, I pleaded, knowing full well that the desperation would lend itself to the other rationally conceived notion of exactly what sort of person I am— the sort who rides on buses, who pays in change, who carries her belongings with her, who doesn't tend to her pets. That was the one that hurt me the most. I couldn't stand the people around thinking that I'd do such a thing as I'd done to Dorian, that I continued to do, forcing him to stay in that

123

terrible cat transport bag, which plagued us all with its putrescence.

Dorian was screaming, and I attempted to comfort him without getting too close. How much did I expect such a small cat to understand? Where had the person gone who used to love him, and how had she turned so quickly into me? The same questions we ask of everyone who's ever done us wrong.

I gave in and started crying.

Might as fucking well.

I grew quickly used to my solitude of attention, in that no one would pay attention to me and I'd therefore be left alone, no matter how many other patrons sat nearby. I looked around each of them and dared they glance back. One girl did, only to be so ashamed of having done so to move seats entirely, toward the back of the bus, away from me and Dorian at the front. I made as if to watch the street closely for my stop, though I knew it would take a little while. So many moments left to live through yet.

I saw Maurice.

He wasn't there, but I saw him in the face of a younger man, politely avoiding staring near the middle of the lines of seats headed toward the rear of the bus. There he was, his looks, his mannerisms. If it weren't for the difference in physical form, I might have thought it was him. Of course, it wasn't.

I belligerently thought of him, anyway.

What might I do, if Maurice were actually here? Would I ask him, please, for help getting to where I was going? We could both get off the bus at some magic stop, where he'd parked a car for just such a purpose, to take us the rest of the way. Of course, he couldn't know where I was going, so I'd have him drop me off at the bus stop, where I had planned to arrive in the first place, stare at him a moment, wait for him to drive off, then continue. But of course, I couldn't do that. I couldn't have Maurice's help anymore, not after all that had happened. And isn't that the brush of it, the fact that now that Maurice had done something to me, now I'm the one that suffers.

CHAPTER 21

What if I could have reacted differently, when I had discovered Maurice's infidelity? What if I had decided at the time, that it wasn't a big deal at all, that it was, in fact, as Maurice had argued, quite fine? What if I weren't the person I am, and the person I could have been didn't fuck everything up, until we ended up here, in the state that we're in?

That's why he couldn't possibly know that anything was awry. Oh, this? I'd say, indicating my bag. A little trip away. The cat? Dorian. He's in need of a little vacation himself. My appearance? A little tumble, nothing to be concerned about, nothing to get upset about, nothing to cry over. The tears? Well, I'd have to wipe those away with something, if to be at all convincing. *But what?* Nothing is clean anymore.

Something from inside the bag.

Of course, something from inside the bag.

I was being ridiculous. I could just change into something from inside the bag before knocking on Dick's door.

I pulled something out from inside the bag and started tending to my face. My foundation would be ruined, but I could push the eye makeup back into some sort of place that made it seem like I'd done it on purpose. A sexy, smoky eye. I imagined Dick Richards looking at my sexy, smoky eye, unbuttoning his trousers, and stroking himself. But now, we would be in the same room, wouldn't we?

Oh god, what if Dick Richards tried to touch me?

All at once, the consequences of existing in physical form in near proximity to Dick Richards overwhelmed me. Of course, he would want to touch me. He may attempt to do so immediately, as soon as the nearness allows for it—as soon as I'm at the door. I imagine showing up to Dick's house, trying to approach from the walkway, and there he strides, out the front door, straight toward me, arms outstretched, and foiling my plans to redress myself. It's so easy to forget the powers someone might hold by existing physically and in near proximity.

It's so easy to take those powers away.

I thought of the safety of my unit, how it wasn't anyone's physical space but mine, how although there were no barriers preventing someone else from entering (there are, after all, doors and windows), still no one *did*, because of the socially constructed barriers, become real through their institutionalization within the organization's mandates. *No employee shall enter the unit of another without explicit invitation and confirmed consent.*

But if someone approached the unit from the outside, one would assume that they did, in fact, want in. And the people who want in, well, we may take all sorts of liberties with them. What if Dick Richards assumed all sorts of things by the bare fact that I approached his domicile?

No. We have a plan for that.

Determined, I pushed the button on the bus to request the next stop. By the time we arrived, I'd be half a block from Dick Richards' physical form.

22

I stood near the back door of the bus ready to exit, my duffel on my shoulder but resting on the seat beside me. Dorian was on the floor. Riding the bus was traumatic enough for him; he didn't need to experience it while tethered to my shoulder. When the bus stopped, I would pick him up and swiftly make my exit. As the vehicle slowed, I again pushed the makeup around my eyes back into place and applied lipstick.

It would have to do.

The bus stopped, and I swiftly made my exit.

I was heartened and enthused at the idea that not all was lost. No matter what tribulations had transpired thus far, I still had an opportunity to make it all right, as long as I made it to Dick's shrub without anyone seeing me. But I was confident, now that I had it all figured out, that this too would work out for me. I would be in the bush in no time, and I conceived of the outfit I would wear.

It was a stretchy black cocktail dress.

Where are you going, dressed like that? Dick Richards wouldn't ask. Dick Richards doesn't care one way or another why I'm wearing what I would be wearing. He would just think it was hot. Now would not be the time at all to start asking questions about my motivations, not when he didn't seem to care at all about them so far in our relationship.

Just as long as I was there.

I looked down at the hem of my pants with scorn but also secure that I would soon be freed of them. They'd go back into the bag to start, but then, into the trash, and in the end, my burdens would be overall lightened. Material goods are just a way of holding people down. They're literal weight, I thought, all the while thinking that the realization would tickle Maurice.

No, I can't think about him now.

It was Dick I should be focused on.

Down the block, I saw the shrub that was my destination. It was grown thick and lush, never losing its leaves in preparation for winter, for such a thing never happened, according to this variety of bush. Or it did, but it was nothing worth shedding one's leaves about. The inner foliage withered as the outer grew each season, emptying out the perfect place for obscuring one's self. It's a wonder no one was living in there already, I thought, briefly considering taking up residence if my plan should fail and I should need somewhere to stay. But I was not an evergreen shrub, and I would need better shelter for the winter.

Entering the open area, actually about human sized, if you didn't move at all, I realized I would have to be careful to avoid catching any of my fabrics on the branches within which, though barren of green, still bore sharp protrusions. A set of tights would be no match for their penetrations, given the right angles of attack.

I set Dorian down first, and then my duffel, searching within for the dress I had pictured. Of course, it would require shapewear, due to the elasticity of the fabric and the impression I intended to make on Dick. But I felt safe enough within the confines of my shrub to believe that, at this time, full nudity would not be a problem, if undertaken with the appropriate vitesse.

As I stripped off the layers of clothes I had on, ensuring that none of it touched the ground or the plant, I thought about Maurice again. I think, he would be proud, knowing that I had escaped the organization once and for all, that I was living free and easy, that I was making new friends and that I was currently stripped to my underwear in the front shrub of a residence in the historical section of town. He would know I was finally free of the confines of my position, the risk of becoming like the people of the organization, almost by accident, just through the length and strength of my previous associations.

As I pulled off my underwear, as it would be better to have fresh on when I met Dick for real for the first time, I thought about our future together, if we even had one. Perhaps once I got to know him a little better, I might decide to free myself of him as well. He held the last vestiges of the organization within my concept of him, and perhaps it would prove too much as, now a free woman, I should not have to even think about them, not any longer. Perhaps I'd not even ring the doorbell; I might just change outfits in Dick's bush and then be on my way, somewhere else. Perhaps I'd be better off alone—a room of one's own, and all that. I had the money saved to live quite a while in the nicest hotel in town. And then I could carry on with Dick if I liked—or not, if I didn't like. I could see what Maurice meant when he said freedom was addictive, that after a while, everything and everyone seemed like a limitation on what was otherwise an infinite potential.

Even the people you love? I had asked him.

Especially the people I love, he had said.

And then I knocked on the door, it opened, and as I saw inside, and what I saw—it was the beginning and the end of everything, the deep well from which springs all hope and all despair. And in that moment, I knew that there had been some grand metaphysical trick played on me, that gods and nature had conspired to bend reality against me, that there was nothing I had known that had ever been certainly true, and that no one, not myself and certainly not Dick, could ever have possibly saved me.

23

Among my reactions, I first noticed the sense of familiarity, the well-ordered way things were arranged, where everyone fit amongst them. I knew this place, even though I'd never been here, because its structure was determined by council at the Building Planning Committee at least 15 years ago, I myself only reading the meeting notes to discern the motivations behind each architectural choice. Inside the door was the office as I remembered it. Before the live and work community, there were individual desks, individual chairs, individuals—and the things that attended them. There were photos of people on the walls, highlights of their accomplishments that hadn't been updated in months, no one having been assigned to audit the public postings such that there they would rest, until some individual worker grew tired of the cluttered space and took it upon themselves to do the work it took to restore it to order. At each workstation sat an individual, their desk adorned with trinkets that *they* owned, that weren't part of the personal belongings assigned to those of us who had taken positions in the units.

At the front desk was Anna Johnstone.

"You made it!" she said first, with measured enthusiasm. And then she made a policy statement: "An employee should dress appropriately for their day."

What the fuck kind of day was I having?

She turned around and walked away, and I had the sense that I should follow her.

"These are your new colleagues. We find it easier to transition to the new office format if the new staff members cut ties with their old colleagues. Thus it was ensured that you would find yourself in trouble at work, isolated, and eventually frustrated enough to make the journey," Anna said, as if she were explaining a new mandate and not destroying my worldview.

Unique scents and perfumes pleasantly assaulted my perception, used as I had become to the sterile environment of the units and more recently, to the sickly smells of public transit and cat urine. Something floral followed something sweet followed something citrus, and I felt alone and out of place, unscented.

"Upper management recognizes the employee's need to express individuality, within limits," Anna went on. "When it became obvious that national trends were moving towards a work-at-home environment, homes were converted into workspaces."

This place was not at all as I had imagined—there was no cozy lighting, no Dick waiting with a bottle of wine, no guest space, no stale linens. Anna's tone turned conspiratorial.

"The employees working from the office have been insisting on access to the units, in order to mitigate the effects of the office environment on their offspring," Anna explained.

"Shouldn't they always have had access to the units?"

"They did, until about six months ago, when the organization clarified that work being done in the office can no longer be attributed to people and has modified the collective agreement to clarify their rights and entitlements."

So that was it. The office people were multiplying and would take over the units, whether the organization wanted it to happen or not, and they were picking the rest of us out one by one, relocating us away from the office people, relinquishing the property to them for the rest of the five-year lease. And then what?

"The units will be repurposed as affordable housing to those already inhabiting it."

"What about my other team?"

"Every individual at the organization is fulfilling an important role. Some of the individuals will remain in the units as support," Anna said. The organization was abandoning them. Anna wanted me to feel like I was one of the lucky ones, moved to a safer environment, but the inequity of it irked me. The lengths they'd gone to ensure I wouldn't catch on and warn them—the incongruency between the policy statement that every individual served an indispensable function but some of them are better off food for mutants. *The differently evolved*, I mentally corrected. My desire to be well-liked at my new establishment conflicted with the overwhelming loss of everything I'd hoped and believed in. I had to ask her.

"What about Dick Richards?"

I waited for Anna to say, *You know Dick? My spouse?* At which point we could have the altercation that I set out here to have. I still imagined that there was a way this move could have been orchestrated where my relationship with Dick carried on in a separate and unrelated fashion, such that it was possible he was real—that it was real—that there was still the option of another life for me.

But instead, Anna said: "There's no such thing."

The way she said *thing* instead of *man*.

"That was a little dramatic," she clarified. "Dick Richards is an integral part of the system, used for a multitude of purposes, and we expect the organization to continue licensing him until the point of obsolescence. I am the lead on Dick's projects while the acting resource advisor is on leave."

The way she described him—Dick is software. I remembered his moans and groans, how predictable his orgasms were, but also everything I'd told him, showed him, how he'd once complimented the symmetry of my labia… it was Anna. Everything I thought I'd gotten away with, part of a period of behaviour modification to prepare me for this—for what? I felt Dick's non-existence like a death I wasn't allowed to grieve, another aspect of the joke.

Maurice's voice in my head: *As long as what you're doing is a reaction to them, even a reaction against, they've got you.*

Where's the other option, Maurice? I looked over the cubicles, everyone's screen supplied with a privacy filter such that its contents couldn't be discerned unless the viewer were looking straight on. I looked at how the space was arranged, such that it was impossible to look straight on, unless the looking was intentional. I heard an employee on a personal call and saw how her colleagues didn't scorn her, neither for the way her voice carried through the workspace nor for the content of her call or the fact that she was using organization equipment and organization time to conduct personal business.

I could have that sort of freedom, I thought. But the idea wasn't enough to assuage my consciousness and the sense that I'd been wronged, that I existed wrongly, and that there was no freedom left to be had in the world. My predicament had become existential. I remembered my arguments with Maurice about how when our freedoms were limited, we still have the freedom to choose which freedom to sacrifice and his response—that our ultimate freedom is to negate freedom all together. To negate choice itself, its preconditions, both the situation and our place within it. It was the framework that led us ultimately to a singularity—the destruction of limits by the destruction of choice by the destruction of the agent—death.

The switch had flipped in my consciousness, and I ran. As Anna meant to lead me through a green painted hallway, past a door marked "Clarifications," I pushed her down and ran back toward the door through which I came, back to Dorian in the bush outside, away from whatever life this was and its crushing sense of inevitability. I ran, and as I ran, I could feel a shift in the draft from the vents as all the heads turned toward me. There's no running at work, no motion that could startle a colleague, no unnecessary bringing attention to oneself, but I broke all those rules in my haste towards the front door of this house turned hellscape. I broke through the door and stood outside for a moment, remembering all the places I couldn't go back to. Not my parents, not Maurice, not the units… I heard Dorian cry; it was getting to be time for dinner. I ran around to the side of the house where I'd left him, crouched, and assured him that it was all going to be all right. People die all the time, and others carry on. I imagined a shot would come at any moment, but when instead I felt a puncture, a heaviness in my back that indicated an object of weight, I was satisfied that at least there would be additional paperwork tomorrow. That my death might matter that much.

EPILOGUE: DORIAN'S SONG

I screamed from inside my chariot.

"Move me! Our bodily fluids are intermingling where I sit!"

But no one listened.

The woman's blood seeped from her wound and stained my carriage. She lay on the ground and, while I could not look her in the eyes, I knew that she had lost the *anima* that made me conscious of her as friend and not as nutriment. Fresh as it was, the smell of her blood sickened me, though I hadn't eaten in days. If it soaked my carriage in an area where there was no urine, even so I'd have a lick.

I screamed again.

There was a man, a woman, and a vehicle whose lights strobed. Their rhythm both soothed and irritated me. I closed my eyes and turned around, as far as I could get from it in my present state of confinement.

I imagine that the woman foresaw her demise and attempted to escape from it. That would explain the long journey we'd undertaken, its many twists and turns, its rumbles and its jostles. The woman would have known something like this was about to occur, and she took me away. But the danger had found her, nonetheless.

There was another woman and a man, both of whom listened only to each other and never to me.

"Were you at all familiar with her?" he asked.

"No, not at all," the woman lied. I could tell by the tone of her voice. It was the same voice my woman used when she teased me. *Did you want something, Dorian? I'm afraid there's nothing here for cats. I'm afraid there's absolutely nothing here for cats.*

There's always something for cats. If the woman were a woman like the woman I used to have, I would soon have another home. I screamed again.

Feed the beast, or I shall burst forth from my stronghold and destroy you!

"Ms. Johnstone, I'm sorry to have to put you through this, but I need to get this down for the record. Please walk me through what happened."

"Well, I heard a noise outside."

"That's when you called emergency services."

"No, that's when I went outside to see what it was. I wouldn't want to waste your time with just a sound."

"Of course not. You checked it out. Go on. You brought the weapon from inside?"

"I had the fork outside the door; I was turning soil earlier this week."

"You brought the gardening tool to confront the noise."

"Yes."

"That settles that. Then you went outside and confronted the victim?"

"I didn't *confront* her. One only confronts things worthy of confrontation. At the time, as I've said, I was very much mistaken about who or what she was."

"You assaulted her without having confronted her."

"No, I'm telling you, one only assaults things they conceive of as worthy of assault."

The tone of it, like when my woman was annoyed after I'd created a "stubborn stain."

"I didn't think it was a human at all. I never would have gone after a human like that. It was fear of what I saw that made me do it."

"And what was it you saw?"

"A hairless coyote in my shrub."

"Please explain for the record."

"I had no reason to think it was a human at all, you see. She was in the shrub. My first thought was that it was an animal. And then when I saw it was hairless, my thought was that not only was there a large animal in my shrub, it was also diseased."

"And that's when you murdered her."

"That's when I killed it. I had absolutely no intention of murdering any *her*."

"I'm sorry to imply that you murdered anyone, Ms. Johnstone. You know I have to ask the tough questions right now, while your memory is still fresh. We both have a role to play here. You're doing a good job. What happened next?"

"The animal let out the strangest sound, as if it had two voices. One reminded me of a housecat, while the other was quite demonic."

"That was probably the woman and the cat," the officer noted.

"Yes, I realize that now. Then, of course, I had no reason to think that the hairless coyote in my shrub had a cat."

"So you called emergency services."

"No," Anna said. "That's when I hit her again. The molting coyote in the bush was suffering, both from disease and from its wound, which I myself had inflicted. So I hit it again, to put it out of its misery."

"Then you called emergency services."

"For a dead coyote? Of course not. Your time is too important."

"Thank you for considering that. When did you call emergency services?"

"I never did. The neighbours called you when they arrived home and saw her in the bush as they were coming up the drive. If they hadn't called, I would have buried it later in the backyard, after my shift."

The tones were like when my woman turned off the talking light box. Something was coming to an end. All had been settled, and it was time to disperse.

But what about Dorian.

"Now there's the matter of the cat, Ms. Johnstone. Now I could call Animal Services, but they're not really taking non-urgent calls in the evenings. Is there any chance you could take it overnight? Now that we know this isn't a crime scene, I think it would be all right to take him inside."

"Of course; you know I love animals."

"Just not hairless coyotes."

"Just not diseased coyotes in my bush!" They both laughed.

"OK, then. That's settled, and thank you for being so accommodating."

"My pleasure," she said, but her tone was too sincere, like there was some enjoyment in it for her, adopting the beloved companion of her victim.

In my new domicile, I shall be appreciated for all that I am and have been.

The new woman picked up my sac and maintained a steady hand as she took me inside and into the bathroom. The other women admired me as well as they could as we passed by. Their sounds indicated I could rely on any one of them for a feeding. We reached the bath and, while I cried, it was a relief to have the water pouring down upon me, my travels having soiled my fine clothes. As she wet, rubbed, and finally rinsed the mixture of bodily fluids down the drain, the new woman hummed.

"I hope you like canned tuna," she spoke to me as she toweled the water away. "We don't have any food for cats." But the way she said it was sincere, because it was true. *A change for the better.* I would have tuna and then a long rest. *Freedom is a full belly and a place to rest.* I understood that the woman would not return, but I also understood that in the world, there are occasionally conflicts, and that such conflicts, the stronger survives the weaker. My new woman would be better able to provide than the last, and as long as no conflict arose between us, I would be free.

ACKNOWLEDGMENTS

Thank you to Sam Richard at Weirdpunk Books, to Ira Rat for the perfect cover design, and to the Void Collective. Thanks always and forever to Rob.

ABOUT THE AUTHOR

Charlene Elsby is a philosophy doctor and civil servant whose books include *Hexis*, *The Devil Thinks I'm Pretty*, *Violent Faculties*, and *Red Flags*. Her essays and interviews have appeared in *Bustle Books*, *The Millions*, and the *LA Review of Books*.

ALSO FROM WEIRDPUNK BOOKS

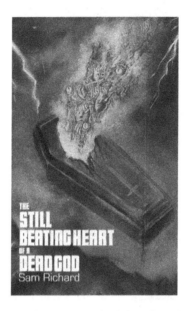

The Still Beating Heart of a Dead God - Sam Richard

A drunk widower wanders through an endless, abandoned mall while the war machine marches.

90s queer metalheads repeatedly try to burn down a regenerating church.

Denizens of a punk house are confronted with the reality of what happened to their missing roommate.

An artist with acidic bodily fluids finds another like him.

With *The Still Beating Heart of a Dead God* Award-Winning author Sam Richard returns with eleven new stories exploring the raw honesty of grief, isolation, brokenness, and desperation through weird horrors ranging from body to cosmic to existential and beyond.

Love Skull - Emma Alice Johnson

Pizza cults! Barn ghouls! Carpet zombies! Skulls and kisses!

A background skull from a popular 80s horror novel comes to life and becomes obsessed with the book's reader. Two women fall in love as a giant monster destroys the town around them. Friends band together to haul their BFF's corpse to the ocean for the ultimate funeral-by-shark.

This collection includes the New York Times-mentioned "5 Ways to Kill Your Rapist on a Farm" and 11 other stories that blend horror, sci-fi, weird, and romance into a unique mix from award-winning author Emma Alice Johnson.

Profane Altars: Weird Sword & Sorcery - edited by Sam Richard

In the spirit of Robert E. Howard, Tanith Lee, Karl Edward Wagner, and films like *Conquest* and *Fire & Ice* comes *Profane Altars: Weird Sword and Sorcery*. Underground horror authors Emma Alice Johnson, Matthew Mitchell, Adam Smith, Sara Century, Charles Austin Muir, Edwin Callihan, and editor Sam Richard conjure forth visions of the unknowable and ancient past. One of spider gods, aging warriors, crystal antlers, cultist soldiers, and whispered legends of strange creatures and woeful knights. A bridge between weird horror and Sword & Sorcery, *Profane Altars* presents new realms fantasy within cloistered worlds of doom and wonder.

Featuring cover art by the legendary Jeffrey Catherine Jones.

Thank you for picking up this Weirdpunk book!
We're a small press out of Minneapolis, MN and our goal is to publish
interesting and unique titles in all varieties of weird horror, often from
queer writers. It is our hope that if you like one of our releases, you will
like the others.
If you enjoyed this book, please check out what else we have to offer, drop
a review, and tell your friends about us.
Buying directly from us is the best way to support what we do.
www.weirdpunkbooks.com